He was going to kiss her.

She *wanted* him to kiss her.

A small voice inside of her begged her to pull back before it was too late. But Meredith knew herself well enough to know that she had never been able to resist Evan, no matter how hard she'd tried. And though years had passed and granted her more self-control where Twinkies and pizza were concerned, it seemed she still had an irresistible weakness for Evan Hanson.

Twelve years.

Evan held a piece of her that had been missing all that time.

Closer, something in her cried to him. *Come closer. Don't let go.*

This time, never let go.

Dear Reader,

This beautiful month of April we have six very special reads for you, starting with *Falling for the Boss* by Elizabeth Harbison, this month's installment in our FAMILY BUSINESS continuity. Watch what happens when two star-crossed high school sweethearts get a second chance—only this time they're on opposite sides of the boardroom table! Next, bestselling author RaeAnne Thayne pays us a wonderful and emotional visit in Special Edition with her new miniseries, THE COWBOYS OF COLD CREEK. In *Light the Stars,* the first book in the series, a frazzled single father is shocked to hear that his mother (not to mention babysitter) eloped—with a supposed scam artist. So what is he to do when said scam artist's lovely daughter turns up on his doorstep? Find out (and don't miss next month's book in this series, *Dancing in the Moonlight*). In Patricia McLinn's *What Are Friends For?,* the first in her SEASONS IN A SMALL TOWN duet, a female police officer is reunited—with the guy who got away. Maybe she'll be able to detain him this time….

Jessica Bird concludes her MOOREHOUSE LEGACY series with *From the First,* in which Alex Moorehouse finally might get the woman he could never stop wanting. Only problem is, she's a recent widow—and her late husband was Alex's best friend. In Karen Sandler's *Her Baby's Hero,* a couple looks for that happy ending even though the second time they meet, she's six months' pregnant with his twins! And in *The Last Cowboy* by Crystal Green, a woman desperate for motherhood learns that "the last cowboy will make you a mother." But real cowboys don't exist anymore…or do they?

So enjoy, and don't forget to come back next month. Everything will be in bloom….

Have fun.

Gail Chasan
Senior Editor

Please address questions and book requests to:
Silhouette Reader Service
U.S.: 3010 Walden Ave., P.O. Box 1325, Buffalo, NY 14269
Canadian: P.O. Box 609, Fort Erie, Ont. L2A 5X3

FALLING FOR
THE BOSS

ELIZABETH HARBISON

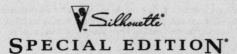

SPECIAL EDITION®

Published by Silhouette Books

America's Publisher of Contemporary Romance

Special thanks and acknowledgment are given to Elizabeth Harbison for her contribution to the FAMILY BUSINESS miniseries.

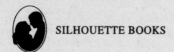

SILHOUETTE BOOKS

ISBN 0-373-24747-8

FALLING FOR THE BOSS

Books by Elizabeth Harbison

ELIZABETH HARBISON

has been an avid reader for as long as she can remember. After devouring the Nancy Drew and Trixie Belden series in grade school, she moved on to the suspense of Mary Stewart, Dorothy Eden and Daphne du Maurier, just to name a few. From there it was a natural progression to writing, although early efforts have been securely hidden away in the back of a closet.

After authoring three cookbooks, Elizabeth turned her hand to writing romances and hasn't looked back. Her second book for Silhouette Romance, *Wife Without a Past,* was a 1998 finalist for the Romance Writers of America's prestigious RITA® Award in the Best Traditional Romance category.

Elizabeth lives in Maryland with her husband, John, daughter Mary Paige, and son Jack, as well as two dogs, Bailey and Zuzu. She loves to hear from readers and you can write to her c/o Box 1636, Germantown, MD 20875.

My thanks to Andre Coutu and James Price, who got me out of my old house. Thanks also to Charles Clark of Waterworks Plumbing in Snow Hill, MD—a true hero in times of need (and leaky pipes and icky bathtubs)— who made my new house so much nicer...and drier.

Prologue

The fact that he actually asked her if she was *really sure* she was ready to do it made her love him all the more.

What other eighteen-year-old guy with a normal libido would be that considerate? Meredith Waters knew—she absolutely *knew*—that if she'd told Evan she wasn't ready, that she was chickening out even though they'd planned this romantic evening together for the past five weeks, he would have backed right off.

He might have needed a cold shower. A really long cold shower. But he would have let her off the hook without the usual guy nonsense about everything from promises broken to the supposedly serious medical consequences of unsatisfied desire.

Guys were, by and large, idiots.

But not Evan Hanson. Evan proved there really were Prince Charmings out there, though they were few and far between. Evan was Meredith's soul mate. She was sure of it. Not that they were the same kind of people—far from it. He was wild and she was conservative. But they complemented each other. And they felt the same way about the most important things. They had the same standards and the same goals for their lives.

Most important, Evan was a guy she knew she could count on through thick and thin. The school and their parents might have thought he was sort of a wild kid, but Meredith knew he'd always be there for her.

Which made her all the more sure that she would never regret what they were about to do. She was a lucky, lucky girl to have her first time be with a guy like Evan.

"Are you sure?" he asked her again, running his hand down the length of her upper arm.

They were lying in her canopy bed, facing

each other. Her parents were out of town for four more days, so not only was the guy perfect but the setting was, too.

She smiled at him, taking in his dark good looks like a tall glass of cold water on a hot day.

And it was definitely hot in here.

"I'm sure," she said, then cocked her head playfully. "But I'm getting the impression *you're* not so sure."

"Oh, I'm sure." He pulled her over to him and kissed her deeply, rolling onto his back so she was on top of him. He wrapped his arms around her tightly, pulling her so close she almost couldn't tell where she stopped and he began.

She loved that feeling.

They kissed and kissed, just like they always did. They'd done it so much at this point that they practically had it down to a science. He moved his mouth this way, she moved her mouth that way, their tongues touched, and—*poof!* Magic.

"I love you, Mer," Evan whispered, slowly rolling her over so she was on her back on the soft mattress and laced-edged sheets she'd bought last month with this moment in mind.

"I love you, too," she said, her response automatic and completely without doubt. "More than you'll ever realize."

He gave that Cheshire-cat grin she adored and reached over to turn off the light on her bedside table.

It took a moment for her eyes to adjust to the light, but when they did she noticed a slash of moonlight cutting through the curtains and spilling onto her bed.

Perfect.

And it was. It was just…right.

Afterward, as she lay in the bed looking out the window while the moon slowly floated higher and crossed the sky like a big silver balloon, she felt more joy than she'd ever felt in her entire life.

Meredith smiled in the dark as Evan talked to her in hushed tones about how beautiful she was and how he wanted to spend the rest of his life with her and how if he didn't get over to the Silver Car Diner for some blueberry pancakes and vanilla cola fast he was going to die.

This, she realized, was perfect contentment.

What she *didn't* realize, in these last few moments of blissful ignorance, was that within two months Evan would be thousands of miles away, without so much as a goodbye, and that he wouldn't look back for more than a decade.

Chapter One

"And that concludes the reading of the will of George Arthur Hanson."

Evan Hanson sat still in the stiff leather chair, feeling like a caricature of the prodigal son, drawn in invisible ink.

He'd returned, as prodigal sons always did, against his better judgment. Instinct had warned him that this would be nothing but trouble—and probably painful to boot—but he'd ignored instinct.

That was a mistake.

His uncle, David Hanson, had been unusually

persuasive in convincing him to come back for the reading of the will. David knew Evan had suffered years of conflict with his father, and that George hadn't spoken to his son since he'd left. Still, David had pointed out to Evan that, while it might be too late to mend fences with his father, he could at least come and hear the patriarch's last message to him and perhaps gain some peace.

It had been peaceful, all right. In fact, his father's message was a resounding silence.

George Hanson had neglected to so much as mention Evan's name in his will, not even to say, "And to my second son, Evan, I leave absolutely nothing. Nada. Zip. Not even a stainless-steel spoon."

It was as if Evan didn't exist to his father.

No, it was worse than that. Evan knew his father well enough to know this lack of mention meant that, to George, Evan really *hadn't* existed anymore once he'd left the country twelve years ago. Since George had effectively run him out of town twelve years ago, that was, by holding the worst kind of emotional blackmail over his head.

Since then, his job presumably done, George had written Evan off, forgotten about him completely.

Everyone knows it's more of an insult to ignore someone than to tell them off. And George had ignored Evan like a champ. They hadn't spoken in twelve years. Sure, Evan could shoulder half the blame for that, but when he'd left he was only eighteen, and his father knew damn well he'd created a situation that made Evan feel as if he couldn't come back.

Surely George should have seen the crisis he'd sent his teenage son into and done something to fix it, or at least make it better. It wasn't in George's nature to extend an olive branch, but even pelting Evan with olives would have been better than the eerie silence.

George hadn't bothered to do anything. He probably hadn't even thought about his middle son more than once or twice in the time between Then and Now.

If only Evan had the same sort of control over his thoughts. He'd have liked to forget his father…and the difficulty of losing his mother when he was seventeen.

And one or two other heartaches—well, one in particular—that had shaped him into the man he was today. A man who wanted nothing to do with his family or with intimate relationships of any sort.

The lawyer closed his books, and Evan's relatives began to discuss the reading amongst themselves, expressing anger at what they had or had not received and at the fact that George had left his young wife full control of Hanson Media Group.

Evan didn't care. It wasn't his problem. None of this was his problem. So with full intentions of leaving it behind forever, he took a deep breath, got up out of his chair and walked purposefully out of the room, planning to keep going until he got to the airport and left American soil for good.

He must have actually convinced himself that no one was aware of his presence because when he heard someone calling his name behind him, at first it didn't register.

"Evan!" It was a woman's voice. One he didn't recognize, though there was nothing surprising about that. It had been more than a decade since he'd heard the voice of anyone in that boardroom.

"Please stop, Evan," she said again. "I'd like to talk to you for a moment."

He stopped and turned to see his father's wife coming toward him in the hallway, a worried expression knitting her flawless features. Her golden hair framed her face as if it had been painted by Vermeer, and her green eyes were bright and alive.

Helen Hanson couldn't have been more obviously a trophy wife if she had been gilded and nailed to a slab of marble.

He'd never met her before—his father had married shortly after he'd left—but, given the circumstances of their meeting now, it wasn't easy to feel any warmth toward her.

"I know you're probably angry about what just happened in there," she began.

"I'm not angry." His tone was cold like his father's, he realized with disgust. "What happened in there—" he gestured toward the room "—is no surprise. In fact, it's absolutely typical of your husband."

She gave a pained nod. "I see why you feel that way, but he was your father, Evan. Don't forget that. Though I know you must feel he rejected you."

He'd thought he'd reached his fill of pain but Helen's words managed to slice deeper still. "I don't *feel* he rejected me, I *know* he rejected me. But don't worry about it, it's not the first time. And knowing how spiteful the old son of a bitch could be, it's probably not the last time, either."

"Evan—"

"He could *always* find a way to express his displeasure with his family." Evan gave a dry laugh. "You might want to watch your own back. Not that you really have anything to worry about. I mean, you *did* get the company."

Helen winced slightly and hesitated before speaking. "Evan, the company belongs to the Hanson family. All of you, not me. It always will."

He gave a dry laugh and looked toward the conference room of the Hanson Media offices, where everyone was still arguing about the outcome of the will. "Try telling that to them."

"They'll find out in time," she answered. Her tone was dismissive of them, but she was looking at Evan intently. "But you—well, it looks like you're not going to stay in Chicago long enough to find out unless someone stops you."

He looked Helen Hanson up and down. She was beautiful—no surprise there—but she also had some nerve. "Is that what you think you're doing? Stopping me?"

She drew herself up and looked him in the eye. "That's what I'm hoping to do."

He shook his head. "Don't waste your effort. I've got no interest whatsoever in what happens to this damned company now."

"But you should," Helen urged. "Don't forget there's a stipulation that twenty percent of the company or company revenues will go to the grandchildren in twenty years."

Evan spread his arms and shrugged. "I realize my father probably didn't tell you much about me, so maybe it's news to you, but I don't have any kids."

Helen's expression softened. "I do know that. But you're only thirty, Evan. You don't know what's going to happen in the future. You might well change your mind."

It was on the tip of his tongue to contradict her, but he'd seen many foolish men make the mistake of banking on their single and childless status, only to be surprised by some turn of events later in life.

"Okay," he said. "I'll grant you that—I don't know what's going to happen. But if I should have kids in the future, they don't need the tainted fortunes of George Hanson, anyway."

She shook her head. "Don't let the sins of your father be visited upon your son." She smiled. Even though it was a small, sad smile, it was dazzling. "Or your daughter, as the case may eventually be."

Evan couldn't see that happening, and it

made him uncomfortable to hear Helen say it, but he didn't argue the case. There was no point. "I'll take my chances," he said, then added half-heartedly, "So will my unborn children."

"Evan, please. Reconsider. Take just a little time. This isn't *just* about the business. It's about your family. Not your father, but your brothers. The whole family is fractured, and they can't heal without you. You're part of them."

He knew he should just walk away, but the woman's desperation intrigued him. Why should she care so much whether a man she'd never met before stayed or went? Surely her husband had told her what a good-for-nothing his middle son was.

"What are you asking me to do?" he asked her.

"I'd like you to stay," Helen said, her voice ringing with sincerity. "I know it probably sounds strange to you, since we don't know each other, but I've got a good feeling about you. I'd like to have your help—actually, Evan, I *need* your help—in returning Hanson Media Group to its former glory."

He hadn't seen *that* one coming. If she hadn't looked so completely earnest, he would have laughed. Instead, he just asked the logical question. "Why me? You've got the whole team on your side." He gestured toward the conference room. "Every one of them has more experience with the company than I do."

Helen glanced behind her and took a step closer to Evan. Her light perfume surrounded her like a protective barrier of…flowers. "But I'm not sure they're going to stay onboard in light of your father's directives. George had a way of manipulating things, you know."

Oh, he knew.

"Anyway," she went on quickly, as if realizing she shouldn't have said that, "I don't know why, but, Evan, I have the feeling I can trust you."

He followed her gaze behind her. No one was there. He almost wished there was someone, though, because he wasn't at all sure he wanted Helen Hanson's confidence. "Look," he said uneasily. "I don't know what you've got in mind, but I can't promise I can do anything to help you."

She sized him up for a moment before saying, "I care about you and your brothers. I truly care about your entire family. Do you believe that?"

He shrugged. "I don't have any reason not to,

I suppose." After all, Helen held all the cards. With controlling interest in the company, she didn't *have* to deal with *any* of the Hansons now. If she was doing so, it was by choice.

Her smile was genuine. "Good. Then trust me when I say that the company *needs* you."

"The company has been doing just fine without me for a lot of years."

"Not really," Helen said. "In fact, the bottom line these past few years has been decidedly bleak."

Evan frowned. "How bleak?"

"Bleak enough that the porn scandal on the Web site was enough to push us firmly into the red."

Jack had e-mailed him—when was it? A month ago? Two?—indicating that the family should get more involved in the business, but Evan had assumed it was just a ploy to get him back into the fold. He'd never imagined that his father had actually dropped the ball and sent the business hurtling toward bankruptcy.

Still, what could Evan do? The only job he'd ever had was running a little beachfront bar in Majorca. And even that could hardly be considered work.

"Well, I'm sorry to hear that, honestly." Evan

shrugged. "But if you're looking to bring the business back to life, you're looking at the wrong guy. I'm not much of a corporate type. It's not just that I don't *want* to help, it's that I honestly don't have anything to offer."

"Maybe not, but you're a risk taker, from what your father told me. And I can tell you're an honest man. He told me that, too. Hanson Media needs that right now."

That stopped Evan. "My father told you that?" He gave a wry smile. "You do know my father was George Hanson, right?"

"He was more fond of you than you know," Helen said, and she sounded as though she really believed it. "He talked about you quite a lot. Said you'd left when you were young and that you'd been living overseas all this time."

"He told you that."

She nodded. "You know, he thought you'd be back. For years he thought you'd come crawling back asking for money, and when you didn't he was secretly impressed."

Evan was embarrassed at the small lump that formed in his throat. He wanted to believe this, even while he still loathed the man and what he'd done to Evan. He wanted, if only for his own peace of mind, to believe that his father hadn't been so detached that he'd just completely *forgotten* him. "Not so impressed that he ever tried to contact me."

"No." A distant look came into her eyes, and she shook her head. "But you know as well as I do that the fact that he didn't contact you had nothing to do with the amount of pride or lack of pride he felt in you. It was all about his *own* pride. *Everything* was about his pride," she added softly.

Evan looked at his father's wife with new eyes. Most women in her position would have been content to let the whole family dissolve so they could regain the money and power for themselves, but Helen was actually reaching out to them.

Now he was left with a choice. He'd already stood here for five minutes talking to her. Five minutes were chipped away from his intended release from the Hanson family. Now he was actually considering Helen's plea for him to stay, and he wasn't sure that was a good idea.

"Look, Helen, what's the upshot here? Give me the bottom line. What exactly are you asking me to do?"

She took a short, bracing breath. "Okay, direct and to the point. I can do that." She met his eyes. "The company is down but it's not out yet. For many reasons I want to fix that. My reasons don't matter that much to you, because you must surely have your own reasons for wanting to stay. It's your legacy. If you have children someday, it's *their* legacy. The time to fix it is now, and I've got a plan. If it doesn't work—" she shrugged "—at least you can't say you didn't try."

"And what do you propose a guy like me, a guy with no business experience whatsoever, should do within this corporation in order to up the revenues?"

"That's easy," Helen replied quickly. "You're smart. A guy with a social conscience and definitely a world view. And, not least, you are a Hanson."

He listened, unable to agree with her for fear of what he'd find himself committing to.

"So what I propose is that you take over the radio division of Hanson Media Group."

He gave a shout of laughter before he realized she was serious.

"The radio division," he repeated, visions of Rush Limbaugh and Howard Stern dancing in his head. "Me."

"Mmm-hmm." She nodded, her green gaze steady on him. "I think you'd be perfect."

"You do know I have no experience in that area whatsoever." He gave another laugh. He couldn't help it. "I wouldn't even know where to begin."

"Given the recent scandal, I think your lack of experience might, in fact, be a plus." She smiled, but there was pleading in her eyes. "I'm only asking you to stay on for three months or so. Just to give it a try. What do you say, Evan? Will you do it? Please."

He thought about it. Majorca would still be there in three months. So would St. Bart's, Fiji or anywhere else he wanted to go. When he'd sold the beachfront bar, he'd made quite a tidy profit. His father would have been surprised to learn that his "beach bum" son was smart enough to invest his earnings.

In any event, he could afford—at least in the monetary sense—to stick around for a little while and see what happened.

The question was, could he afford the mental toll it would undoubtedly take on him to stay?

Suddenly the words of his uncle, David Hanson, came back to him. David had been trying to convince Evan to come back and mend fences with his father several months ago, before it was too late.

Think about it, Evan, David had said. *You don't need to do this for George. You need to do it for yourself.*

Those were the words that had brought Evan back, even though he'd arrived too late. They were the words that had rung in his mind when he'd contemplated seeing his siblings again. Who knew where life would take them eventually? Right now they were all here, working together toward a common goal, and he had the opportunity to help with that.

Granted, failure was possible. All he could do was his own personal best. If someone couldn't accept him or forgive him, he didn't have to carry it.

"Okay," he heard himself saying to Helen, despite the fact that it went against every instinct he felt in his gut. Instinct that told him to run like hell and never look back. "I'll do it."

Chapter Two

"What I'm looking for is someone to work in advertising and public relations under my brother-in-law," Helen Hanson was saying to the young brunette woman before her.

Meredith Waters sat uncomfortably in the plush chair opposite Helen's sleek, modern desk, wondering if it was appropriate or wildly *in*appropriate to mention her history with the Hanson family before this job interview with Hanson Media went any further.

She *never* thought she'd set foot in the company George Hanson had built. Not after what he'd done to her family.

"I think you'll agree, the benefits are generous," Helen went on, handing a folder across the desk to Meredith. Her hand was delicate and smooth, her manicure perfect. Helen Hanson was perfectly turned out.

Meredith glanced at the folder, so it at least looked as if she was interested. Medical, dental, two weeks' vacation time, two weeks' personal time…yes, the terms were extremely generous. A person would have to be a fool to turn this down.

Of course, Meredith would have taken the job no matter what, even if it had paid minimum wage and offered the single benefit of a half hour's lunch once a week. Pretending to hesitate was just that—pretending.

It was all a game.

She just hoped she could play it without anyone finding out.

"I'd like to think about it," Meredith lied. She didn't need to think about it. She was ready to start now. "Could I take a day or two and get back to you?"

Helen looked uncertain. "I'd really like to fill the position as soon as possible. As you're undoubtedly aware, I've only just come back myself." She gestured at some of the packed boxes that were piled in the corner. "Plus, we have a major scandal we're still trying to clean up, and there's a lot of work to do. If you're unsure of your interest, that's fine, but please understand I'll have to keep interviewing."

Clearly, Helen was a master at this game.

Meredith tipped her head slightly. "You sure know how to make an offer a person can't refuse."

"Does that mean you accept my offer?"

"Yes." Meredith smiled and held her hand out. "You've got yourself a deal, Mrs. Hanson."

"Helen, please." Helen shook her hand, looking delighted. "I'm so glad to have you on board, Meredith. Now, you'll be working under my brother-in-law, David Hanson, in the PR department, but I'd like you to focus special attention on the radio division that's now being run by my late husband's son, Evan Hanson."

Whoa! This was *not* the plan.

"I'm sorry, did you say *Evan* Hanson?" Meredith asked, feeling as though Helen had just punched her in the stomach.

Helen nodded absently, taking a narrow silver pen out of her drawer. "Mmm-hmm. My middle stepson, Evan."

Meredith cleared her throat. "Forgive my saying so—perhaps the newspapers were wrong—but it was my understanding that Evan Hanson had shunned the family business and moved away. A long time ago." Twelve years, if memory served correctly.

Helen jotted a note on a pad next to her and returned her attention to Meredith. "Yes, he was. But he's back now, working with all of us to make Hanson Media the most successful business it can be." She raised an eyebrow at Meredith. "That's not a problem, is it?"

"N-no. I'm just not sure I understand." Meredith had to back off. She didn't want to look as if a person in the company could be her Achilles' heel. "You want me to concentrate my efforts entirely on *one* division rather than the whole company?" This wasn't what she'd had in mind when she took this job.

But now she was already committed.

"It should be an exciting challenge," Helen said, hopefully unaware of the tension that was building in Meredith. "I think you'll enjoy it. Yes, there will be some initial difficulties, perhaps, but once you and Evan start working together, everything should work out just fine. I have a feeling about it."

What was she, psychic? Did she know something more than she'd revealed in the interview?

"I have to say, I'm not used to dealing with radio," Meredith hedged, feeling a little frantic and trying to keep it out of her voice. "You might do better to have me learn the ropes there part-time while I'm also working other areas."

"Don't worry," Helen said lightly. "Evan's not used to doing anything with radio. I think, in this case, it will serve you well. Bob Smith had years of experience, but he couldn't make a viable go of that division. So now it's a blank canvas for you and the rest of the team to paint whatever future you want."

Normally that would be a very appealing offer. Not this time, though. "Still, it's hard to get by without *any* experience. I might be more of a detriment than an asset to a division I know nothing about."

Helen was clearly unconcerned. "You and Evan will both have a very strong support staff under you, but I think this inexperience you're concerned about is *exactly* the thing that's going to help you think outside the box. Both of you."

Meredith swallowed, but the lump in her throat wouldn't go away. Nerves. She'd always had trouble with them. "Okay, Mrs.— Helen.

Okay, Helen." She didn't want to do it, but she had no way out. "I'll give it my best shot."

Helen smiled broadly, revealing even white teeth and the kind of looks usually reserved for the covers of magazines. "Great, Meredith! I'm *so* glad to have you with us. I just know you're going to do a terrific job."

"Thanks very much. I'm thrilled to take it on." In truth, Meredith wished she shared even half of Helen Hanson's enthusiasm.

Unfortunately, all she felt now was a lot of insecurity about her job performance…and that was something she was definitely *not* used to struggling with.

It wasn't just the job parameters: she knew how to do her work, regardless of the details. All of that had been laid out quite clearly for her, and she was comfortable in the knowledge that she could do it, and do it well.

What worried her was doing her job well when she had to do it so close to the man who'd dumped her without a backward glance.

Helen told Evan she'd hired someone new for the PR department, someone who would concentrate their efforts on promoting the new face of Hanson Broadcasting. He was glad of that, because, with the support of the previously existing staff, he'd managed to contact three notorious on-air talents, two of whom had already signed on, but he was at a complete loss about what to do to promote them.

That was where the PR department came in. They were, after all, the professionals. Radio should be easy for them. A contest here, a print ad there, that should do it. Radio was free; it sold itself. Evan's meeting with David's underling should only be informative, involving the plans they already had for promotion of the radio division.

At least, that was what Evan thought. Until David's underling actually appeared at his office for their one o'clock appointment.

Meredith Waters.

Gleaming chestnut hair, with tinges of red that shone like copper in the sunlight; pale Irish skin that she'd inherited from her mother; green eyes; and a wide, generous mouth. Evan had never seen a smile so bright that could turn, in an instant, to a heart-aching sensuous curve that would drive any man to distraction.

He would have recognized her anywhere, anytime, even though he hadn't seen her in… well, twelve and a half years. It was marked indelibly in his mind since it was the night he'd left the United States.

The night of their senior prom.

He hadn't actually made it *to* the prom, of course, which was one of the reasons this meeting now was so…awkward.

The last time he'd seen Meredith Waters, it had been through her bedroom window as she'd sat in front of her vanity mirror, putting the final touches on her makeup and hair for a prom date that wasn't going to show up.

Evan.

The image had haunted him ever since. Meredith, in a thin-strapped deep-blue dress, her pale shoulders creamy and tempting. He could feel the curve of them in his empty hands.

Even then, but certainly now, he recognized what a sweet, innocent beauty she was. Hers had been a difficult life, with a lot of hard knocks, despite her best efforts. Her parents, too, had suffered at the hands of fate, and, unfortunately, at the hands of George Hanson, even though they were good people who deserved better.

Evan thought she'd do better without him around.

Apparently, it hadn't turned out that way. And

by the time he knew what had happened, it was far too late for him to come back and make things better.

He wished he'd had the advantage of wisdom then that he had now.

Instead of rising to the occasion, he'd left. It was soon after his mother had died, and the rawness of that loss probably contributed to his confusion. No one to run interference for him. No one to offer even an iota of warmth to the house that had never entirely felt like home.

Evan knew if he'd stayed he would have gotten as bitter and mean as the old man—they were so much alike in other ways it was practically a shoo-in—so rather than doing that to Meredith and himself, he'd just moved on.

Until this moment he hadn't stopped to regret his decision.

"Hello, Evan," she said, her voice smooth and modulated. It was familiar but, at the same time, unfamiliar. "It's been a long time."

He was as paralyzed with surprise—no, *shock*—as he would be if he'd been looking at a ghost. In a way, in fact, he felt like he was. He felt like he should say something profound, but only one word came to mind.

"Meredith?"

She nodded, but no smile touched that beautiful mouth. "You recognize me."

"Of course I recognize you. You look…" *Beautiful. Stunning.*

Haunting.

"You look the same as you always did." But she didn't. She didn't look the same at all. She looked like a sleek, sophisticated version of her old self.

This was awkward. Really awkward.

But Evan still didn't know what to say. Unfortunately the momentary uncomfortable pauses weren't buying him enough time to come up with something pithy.

She smiled. And for just a moment, he could see the high-school girl inside the woman.

"Clearly you weren't expecting to see me." There wasn't a trace of self-consciousness in her voice. "I was hoping Ms. Hanson would have let you know I was coming."

This wasn't making any sense. "Ms. Hanson?"

"Yes, Helen Hanson." Meredith nodded. "She just hired me in PR and has asked me to assist you in promoting this division."

A pause dropped between them like a tennis ball and bounced awkwardly into several silent seconds.

"Are you serious?" he asked after a moment. How was this possible? Of all the people Helen could have hired, and all the places within the company she could have placed a new employee, how on earth had it happened that she'd hired Meredith and wanted her to work with Evan?

Meredith's smile froze a little. "Yes. Will that be a problem for you?"

Damn right it was a problem. It was hard enough to be back in Chicago and working in the Hanson offices. He was running up against memories—including lots of unpleasant ones—at virtually every turn.

But this? This was too much.

"No, it's not a problem at all," he lied. Then he forced what he hoped looked like a casual smile, though it felt more like he was grimacing. "I'm sorry, I must seem rude. It's just that it's been more than twelve years since I've been in Chicago, and I'm still trying to orient myself. Needless to say, I've been seeing a lot of people I haven't seen in a long time and it's disconcerting each time I get one of these blasts from the past."

"I understand," Meredith said, her tone cool, professional. Clearly she'd grown far, far beyond the awkward kid he'd once known. She was detached in her interaction with Evan now. It was very clear that this wasn't personal for her.

Hell, maybe she didn't even remember what they'd once been to each other.

For that matter, maybe he'd imagined it. Maybe this thumping in his chest at the sight of her was just the remembrance of a dream he'd once had. His life had taken so many surreal turns at this point that he wasn't sure of anything at the moment.

"I do hope we'll be able to get past any awkwardness and work effectively together," Meredith went on, but for the first time her voice betrayed the merest trace of a waver.

"Absolutely."

"Good. So let's get to work on our plan to raise the profile of Hanson Broadcasting." She glanced at her watch. "Do you have time to talk about it now? I'd like to get up to speed on your plans so I can start my work as soon as possible."

There was no way Evan could just leap into this now. He needed a little time to collect his thoughts.

He'd begun outlining a mission already, of course, but it would have taken some time to prepare to discuss it even if it *wasn't* Meredith waiting for it, but the fact that it was... Well, he just needed a little time to get used to the idea.

"I'm about to have a meeting," Evan said, trying to sound regretful rather than unprepared. "Are you free later this afternoon?"

Meredith shook her head. "I told David I'd be available to talk to him this afternoon."

Another pause spread between them.

"So maybe tomorrow—" Evan began.

"I *am* available at lunch," Meredith suggested at the same time.

They looked at each other for a second before Evan said, "Lunch is fine."

"Okay, great."

"How about the Silver Car Diner around noon?"

The Silver Car Diner. As soon as the words were out of his mouth he regretted them. That was a place they'd been to together quite a few times in high school. In fact, it was his former familiarity with the place that made it the first thing out of his mouth, yet he couldn't have picked a more pointedly sentimental place unless he'd suggested the backseat of his ancient Chevy Monte Carlo.

Before he could retract the offer and suggest

something less personal, Meredith, with what could have been a look of surprise in her eyes, nodded and said, "Okay. Sounds fine."

"Great." Evan reached for some papers to straighten. "See you there at noon."

She gave a small smile and nod and turned to leave. Evan continued to straighten his pile of papers, half watching her go, until she was finally down the hall and out of sight.

Working with her wasn't going to be easy.

Meredith had felt Evan's eyes on her as she'd walked away. For a moment or two she'd actually worried that she might trip or stumble, betraying her nervousness.

How in the world was she going to work with Evan Hanson? It was preposterous! If she wasn't already so committed, she would have walked away from the job the moment she knew he was involved. But a lot of people were counting on her. This went far deeper than mere PR for Hanson Media Group.

Before she'd agreed to this job, she'd done some investigating and learned that Evan was hopping all over Europe and the Caribbean. She'd actually taken the care to make *sure* he wasn't going to be around if she had to get involved in his family business. It never even occurred to her that he might end up coming back to Hanson Media Group—which she knew he'd always disliked—the moment she was hired.

If someone had offered her a bet, she would have bet everything she had that he wasn't going to be there.

"Everything all right?" David Hanson asked her when she got back to their promotions.

"What? Oh, fine. Fine. I was just thinking about something."

David looked skeptical. She'd already learned he wasn't an easy one to fool. "You sure?" he asked. "There's nothing I can do to help?"

She smiled at him. "Actually, I could use some information on how the television stations have been doing over the past year or so."

He looked puzzled. "I thought you were working with Evan on the broadcasting division."

"I am," she said quickly. "But I think it will be helpful to know how Hanson Media is doing in other arenas. Maybe we can learn from other divisions' successes and mistakes."

David gave a dry laugh. "Hanson Media Group isn't doing all that great in any area, but the fact is, the television division is doing nicely. We've produced an original medical drama that's done really well, and also the reality show *Run for Your Life* will be back this fall."

"Ah." Meredith nodded and made a mental note. "That's in its third or fourth season now, isn't it?"

"Fifth."

Five seasons. That was pretty solid. Her employer would be pleased to hear it. "And are the advertising revenues for those shows on par with some of the other popular mainstream network shows?"

"Absolutely. In fact, last year *Run for Your Life* aired after the Super Bowl, and the advertising went really well. You might want to talk to Bart Walker about that if you want the details. I'm not sure it really correlates to the radio division but it might give you some ideas."

She smiled and nodded. "I'm very interested in getting details about the whole company," she said. "The more information I can get, the better I can do my job."

David studied her keenly and nodded. "That sounds good. We have an administrative assistant named Marla who's ace at doing just about any research you can think of. You might ask her to gather some facts for you."

Meredith fully intended to do all of her own research, but she didn't want to stand out in any negative way to David, and she especially didn't want to look like a know-it-all. Particularly since she knew more than she should about the workings of the company already.

"Thanks for the tip," she said, smiling and heading for her office. "I will definitely make a point of contacting her this afternoon."

"That reminds me," David said, apparently unsuspicious. "I'm going to be out this afternoon, so if you have any questions, you can get me on my cell phone."

Meredith took a sharp breath and glanced behind her, half afraid that Evan might be there and catch her in a lie about meeting with David in the afternoon.

But of course he wasn't there. No one was.

"Don't worry about a thing," she assured David, hoping her duplicity didn't show on her face. "I can feel my way around or find someone to help if I need to. It won't be a problem." She tried to project absolute confidence, though she was feeling anything but. "No problem at all."

Chapter Three

Why had he picked the diner, of all places?

He probably just wasn't thinking about it, Meredith decided. Perhaps it didn't have the same ring of melancholy for him that it did for her. Not that it was a *huge* deal or anything. After all, it had been years since they were together, and the fact that he had been her first lover probably gave the relationship far more weight in her memory than in his. Twelve years had passed, yet some memories felt like yesterday.

* * *

"I love you, you know," eighteen-year-old Evan had said to seventeen-year-old Meredith as they walked into the Silver Car Diner at 3:00 a.m. for a late-night snack.

"I thought you did." She smiled, still languishing in the afterglow and warmth of his touch, despite the cold outside. "Otherwise I never would have…you know. Done what we just did."

"Neither would I."

"Liar."

He smiled, that gorgeous devil smile that made her heart flip every time. "Maybe I would have," he conceded.

"You would." She smiled, privately secure in the wholehearted belief that he *did* love her, and nothing else mattered.

He echoed her thoughts. "Okay, but it doesn't matter because I *do* love you."

"I love you, too, and you know it," she said, thrilling at the feel of the words tripping off her tongue. She'd been with Evan for over a year now, but she still felt the tickle of infatuation. That, she decided, was how she knew this was real love.

Evan squeezed her hand, and a tired-looking waitress led them to their favorite booth in the corner and took their orders for blueberry pancakes and colas.

When she had gone, Evan put money in the jukebox. Their eyes met and, as was their custom, he pushed a random letter and she pushed a random number and they listened to see what would play.

This time it was Jerry Lee Lewis singing "Breathless."

Perfect.

"So you know what I'm thinking?" Evan asked.

"Probably the same thing you're always thinking," Meredith answered with a giggle. "But can we take a break to eat first? I'm starving. And it wasn't a half hour ago that you told me you were going to die if you didn't come here and eat some blueberry pancakes." She gave a mock sigh of exasperation. "Even Don Juan took a break *sometimes.*"

He rolled his eyes. "That wasn't what I was going to say. I mean, I'm all for that, but I was going to say I think maybe we should get married after we graduate."

Her breath caught in her throat. Thrills filled her like bubbling champagne. "College, you mean."

He shook his head. "High school. Why not? If we know that's what we're going to do anyway, why wait?"

A voice somewhere in her warned that this

might not be a good idea, but at the moment she couldn't think why not. "Graduation is in two months!"

"Great." He reached across the formica tabletop and took her hands in his. "The sooner, the better. Let's make your prom dress a wedding dress instead."

"Come on."

"Fine, we'll go to the prom and you can wear something else for our wedding. What do you say?"

Meredith would have run off with him right this minute but someone had to be the voice of reason here, didn't they? "What would we do about jobs? A home?"

He shrugged. "Whatever we'd do anyway. We could stay and work here, of course, but what about that trip to Greece? Why not just go and stay a year? We could work in a bar at night and just lie in the sun all day long, doing whatever we want. *Whenever* we want," he added meaningfully.

She sighed. It sounded like heaven.

"Seriously, Mer, I would talk to your parents right now if they were in town."

She gave a laugh. "If they were in town, we wouldn't be here. And we wouldn't have been able to—" she hesitated "—do what we did tonight."

He twined his fingers in hers, and looked deep into her eyes. "And we wouldn't be able to go back to your house and spend the whole night together."

Spend the whole night together. She turned the idea over in her mind. She could sleep in Evan's arms and wake up with him, seeing his eyes and his smile before anything else in the morning.

God, she loved him.

"I wish it could be like this every night."

"It can," he insisted. "It will. You'll see."

But Meredith was always skeptical of things that seemed too good to be true. There was always something deep inside her warning her that she might be disappointed. "I hope so," she had said wistfully.

Instead of answering, Evan had kissed her.

At the time, she had taken that kiss as reassurance. A promise that would be kept.

Now she knew better.

As Evan and Meredith entered the restaurant together to discuss the mundane details of Hanson Media, the familiar smell of cheeseburgers and waffles drifted into Meredith's senses, and she had to remind herself to be as professional and as aloof as she could be.

It was hard to forget the past they shared here, but if Evan could be cavalier about it, she would, too. Since they had no choice but to work together, she needed to be very careful not to add undue discomfort to the situation.

"Man, this smell takes me back," Evan said, inhaling deeply as they followed a pink-uniformed hostess to a booth along the back wall. "This is one thing I really missed when I was overseas." He gave a laugh. "It's hard to find blueberry pancakes and wet fries in Europe."

Meredith thought he'd lost a lot more than diner food when he'd left, but she didn't say so. "I'll bet," she said, sitting down opposite him on the cold vinyl seat. She felt like a poorly cast actress in a play about her own life. "But I'm sure Europe had its perks."

"Yeah, chief among them being that it wasn't here." He looked at the small jukebox on the wall of the booth and shook his head. "Good Lord, they've still got Jerry Lee Lewis on here. You'd think they'd have updated that."

"The jukebox only runs 45s," Meredith pointed

out, sounding didactic and snooty even to her own ears. "It's not like you can just stick CDs in it."

He looked at her with amusement in his eyes. "I left the country, Meredith, I didn't leave the planet. I know how a jukebox works." He smiled. "Though they do make CD ones now." He reached into his pocket and produced a handful of change, which he dropped on the table with a clatter. "Still a quarter?"

She glanced at the box and felt for a minute as if she was watching a movie of her own life. How many times had they been here together? She'd probably studied the jukebox in this very booth before. Multiple times. It was a quarter. It was always a quarter here.

If only the rest of life were so consistent.

"You okay?"

His question startled her back into the moment.

"Yes, fine," she said. "I was just thinking about work."

"This ought to change that." He put the quarter in and hesitated for just a fraction of a second before pressing C and 7 at the same time. "Get you thinking about math homework instead," he added with a small laugh.

The sound of an old Platters song drifted

out of the small, tinny speakers. Meredith knew it because it had been one of her grandfather's favorites.

Evan had known that once. Was it too presumptuous to think that was why he'd chosen it this time?

"You're not the only one with a memory," he said, as if in answer to her unspoken question.

"What do you mean?" she asked. Where Evan was concerned, her rule was going to be Assume Nothing.

He gestured toward the jukebox. "You picked this song about a million times."

She repositioned herself, hoping her straightened posture would pass for a lack of sentimentality. "That's funny, I don't really remember that."

"Yes, you do."

"What?"

He cocked his head and said, "We have a past, Meredith. There's no getting around it, no matter how much you might want to. We can't pretend we don't know each other."

"We don't," she said, too quickly. She sounded defensive. She *was* defensive.

She was going to have to get some perspective.

He shrugged and fiddled with a sugar pack

from the little container on the table. "We did once."

"What did we have, Evan?" She looked him squarely in the eye, even though it made her feel weak inside. "Obviously, it wasn't that close, or that special, because you up and left it without so much as an *adiós*."

"That wasn't because of you, Meredith."

If she'd been successful at pretending non-chalance at all, she lost it then. "I didn't know *what* it was about."

"It was just…me. My own stuff. I'm sorry if it hurt you."

That was it? After all these years, that was what she got in the way of retribution? *I'm sorry if it hurt you.*

Like there was some possibility that it hadn't.

Like maybe she hadn't even noticed, at seventeen, that the boy she adored more than anything on earth—the guy she was sure she was going to spend the rest of her life with—had just disappeared into the night. Lord, she'd been so sure—so wrong, but so darn sure—about his feelings for her that for the first six months she had continued to insist that something must have happened to Evan.

Imagined him wounded somewhere, needing

help…. Thoughts had plagued her, night and day. She couldn't eat, couldn't sleep, couldn't focus.

And now he was sorry *if* he'd hurt her?

"It wasn't just about you," she said quietly, holding her outrage and disbelief deep inside.

"What do you mean?"

If he didn't know, she didn't want to have to explain it to him. It was all such old news now, anyway—how could she talk about it without sounding like a desperate loser who had been stuck in the past for all this time?

How could she explain what it was like for her—the girl who had trusted, and given of herself, and who thought if there was one thing in the world she could count on it was Evan Hanson—to find out that everything she'd thought was real for two and a half years was just an illusion? And even that revelation had come only after she'd gone through the undue stress of fearing the worst.

It sounded small to the disinterested audience, yet to Meredith it had been a life-shaping experience.

"What I mean is, we need to keep this about business," she clarified. "Whatever we had was over a long time ago. And opening old wounds isn't going to achieve anything positive or productive for either one of us."

"Right."

She went on, "Like I said, we don't know each other anymore, and if we move forward acting like we do, based on ancient information, it's just counterproductive."

He hesitated, studying her, then said, "Okay, then. Business, not personal. Got it." He pushed the menu aside. "I already know what I want, how about you?"

She knew she wanted to get out of there as quickly as possible, so she pushed her menu to the end of the booth with his. "I'll just get a cheeseburger."

"Medium well, cheddar cheese, no raw onions, right?" Evan didn't smile, but he may as well have. His eyes clearly showed that he had won a point.

And her heart conceded that point privately. Though she wouldn't have wanted to admit it to Evan—or anyone else, for that matter—she hadn't changed so much since she was a teenager. Basically Meredith Waters had always been the same person—she had simple tastes, a good work ethic and she could be counted upon to take the slow-but-steady route.

The only real difference, and it had come courtesy of Evan himself, was that now she had a very cautious heart.

Meredith Waters was determined to never fall in love again.

Chapter Four

"You're consistent," Evan said to her, having predicted her order. "That's a good thing."

"You're right." She looked at him evenly. "It's a quality I've really grown to appreciate in people."

He paused, then said, "But you don't mean that personally, right?"

"Right. It was just a general comment." She didn't sound convincing, even to her own ears, so when the waitress appeared to take their orders, she was glad for the interruption.

As soon as the woman turned away, Meredith

tried to put the conversation back on track, or at least get it off the track it was on. "So let's talk about your plans for Hanson Broadcasting. I understand you're planning to change the format to all talk?"

There was a moment's hesitation before he followed her into that line of conversation. "It's hard to do anything unique in music radio these days, but with talk we can corner the market if we get or develop popular talents."

"But there's a lot of danger in that, too," Meredith pointed out, comfortable to be back on less intimate turf. *This* she could talk to him about. This she could talk to *anyone* about. "As soon as I heard you wanted to switch to talk, I did some research. Almost every radio network that's succeeded with talk has done so with shock jocks." She hesitated, waiting for him to interject, but he just nodded, so she continued, "And though there's reward potential, the risks tend to be high. Too high." Especially given her current job description, though she didn't add that. It would be awfully hard for her to do a good job if she was trying to put out obscenity fires all the time instead of gathering pertinent information about Hanson Media Group.

"What risks are you referring to?" Evan asked.

She chose her words carefully. "A lot of these DJs have trouble toeing the line. They want to be outrageous so people talk about them and listen to them."

Evan shrugged. "If we want ratings we need people who are willing to push the envelope."

Meredith frowned. It sounded as if things she thought were dangers were assets to him. "Which envelope are you planning on pushing and exactly who do you have in mind for the job?"

He tapped his fingertips on the gray-and-white tabletop. "Envelopes, any. I don't care. Who do I have in mind? Several people. I already secured the Sports Addicts, Bill Brandywine and Zulo Gillette. But the biggest coup is that I've already talked to Lenny Doss about coming here for the morning-drive hours. I think I can get him onboard."

Suddenly it felt like the air-conditioning had gotten very cold. "Lenny Doss," Meredith repeated. His name had come up quite a few times in her research. So had the Sports Addicts, and though they weren't her cup of tea, they were essentially harmless. "You've got to be kidding."

"Nope." He looked quite pleased with himself. "All it took was the right offer."

Alarm bells were going off in her head and he was oblivious. "Evan, you can't hire Lenny Doss."

That got his attention. "Why not?"

Did she really need to spell this out? "The guy is a major liability. The last company that hired him ended up paying the FCC more than half a million bucks in fines."

Evan nodded with apparent understanding. "You're referring to him dropping the F-bomb on the air."

"No—well, yes, but not *just* that." She couldn't even imagine trying to clean up after Lenny Doss. "He also had his listeners go to the Washington Monument and—"

Evan put his hand up. "I know all about that. You're right, it's inexcusable, but it's not going to happen again."

She couldn't believe he knew this stuff and still wanted to hire the guy. "Evan, if you hire Lenny Doss, you are in danger of putting the final nail in the coffin of Hanson Media Group."

He looked at her and she noticed his jaw was tensing the way it always had when he was frustrated.

Evan Hanson didn't like being told he couldn't do something. Never had.

"I'm aware of the dangers," he said. "This

business may be new to me, but as soon as Helen put me on the job, I did my research, and I surrounded myself with some pretty knowledgeable people."

"I'm not saying you can't do your job," she said. "I'm saying…" What was she saying? How could she finish that sentence without coming off more adversarial than she already had? "That if you do this, you're going to make it hard for *me* to do *my* job."

Evan looked at her evenly, then smiled and said, "Tactful recovery."

Fortunately, they were interrupted by the arrival of their food.

"That was fast," Meredith commented gratefully as the young redheaded busboy set a plate down with a clatter in front of her. A French fry fell off and landed next to the plate, leaving a small splatter of gravy on the formica.

"I'm sorry," the kid said quickly, reaching to clean it up and nearly knocking her glass of ice water into her lap.

"It's okay, don't worry about it," she said quickly, noticing Evan pushing her plate a little to the side before the kid accidentally knocked into it, too.

Funny how they could be a good team in such

a small way, or at least work in harmony to save a plate, and yet they disagreed about virtually everything of any importance.

"We'll take it from here," Evan said in a way that was distinctly dismissive.

"Thanks," Meredith added to the kid.

The busboy left and Evan turned his attention back to Meredith. "I could almost swear that same kid worked here when we used to come." He smiled, and Meredith's heart did a stupid flip. "He looks like he hasn't aged a day."

She couldn't help smiling back. "There's always a kid like that working in places like this. I think they hire them from central casting."

They laughed and for just a moment the tension was lifted from the conversation. It was back a moment later, though, when Evan said, "Now, where were we?"

Meredith picked at her French fries. "I believe I was trying to get you to see how crazy it would be to hire Lenny Doss and you were being bullheaded about it."

"Ah, yes." He smiled again. The tension in the air between them lessened a bit. "You don't mince words."

"Not when I'm this serious about something."

He let out a long breath. "Look, Meredith,

there's also the chance that it will work, and it will raise the profile of Hanson Media Group in a really positive way. The business world needs to take us seriously and this could do it."

"I agree with your theory, but I'm not so sure about your methods," she said. "Are you willing to do this and take the chance of it blowing up in your face?" The air conditioner kicked off halfway through her sentence, and Meredith realized she was practically yelling to be heard. "Do you really want to be the one to blow this for your whole family?" she finished in a lower voice.

Evan tapped his fingers on the table again, louder, faster. His whole face—a face she'd once known so well, but which, at this moment, seemed like a stranger—pulled into a frown. Even his eyes appeared to darken. "Yes, Meredith, I guess I am willing to take that chance. And, with all due respect, I don't think it's your job to worry about it."

"But that's *exactly* what my job is. My department already has its hands full trying to salvage the image of Hanson Media Group from the whole porn scandal. Adding Lenny Doss to the mix is like trying to put a fire out with gasoline."

Evan shook his head and took a big bite of his hamburger, looking unperturbed.

Understanding began to dawn in Meredith's mind. "Oh, my God. You don't care, do you?"

He raised an eyebrow in question.

But it wasn't really in question. She'd seen this gesture before. It was an invitation for her to tell what she knew so he could either confirm or deny.

"You don't care if the whole company goes under," she went on, half to herself and half to him. "If you succeed, you're all right with that, but if you fail…" She studied his face. "My God, Evan, if you fail, you don't care about that, either, do you?"

The moment of silence that passed between them seemed so long that she felt as if she'd sat staring at him for five minutes, listening to the clanking of utensils and plates and the shouts and laughter around them. It was a standoff and he wasn't backing down.

Well, neither was she.

"You always were afraid to take a chance, weren't you?" Evan said finally.

"What?"

"You're saying I shouldn't do this because it's risky. I think that's coming from a personal bias on your part. You've always been afraid to take a risk."

She thought of the risks she'd taken with him. The ultimate risks she'd taken in giving him her virginity and entering the kind of intimacy she could never erase. "I've taken a few."

It didn't appear that he took her meaning. "As I recall, you were as straitlaced as they come, always playing by the rules. Even in science class, instead of switching the chemicals up a little bit to see if we could make flubber or something, you insisted on following the program." He made it sound like an insult.

But she was proud of having played by the rules in high school. It was easy to cheat, to lie and to deceive—she'd found that out later on. "Yes, I preferred to use the method that worked, that was tried and true. It's just good sense."

"Good thing Thomas Edison didn't feel that way." He took another bite of his burger.

How could he eat at a time like this? Meredith couldn't even think about her food. "Oh, for heaven's sake, you're not trying to invent the lightbulb, you're just trying to hire a proven jerk to put on the air so you can have the sublime pleasure of watching your family business explode like a firecracker."

"That's not true," he protested, gesturing at her with his burger. "I am not *trying* to make the company go under. Despite what you think, I *do* care. I'm trying to help. But you're right— if it doesn't work out, it's not going to be the end of my world."

"So you're willing to put everyone's future on the line." She felt the tug of an anger she hadn't felt in a long time. "And if things don't go the way you want them to, you'd rather bail on everyone who cares about you—no matter how much it hurts them—than do a little hard work to try and get along."

He winced. She was almost sure of it. "That's an easy explanation, isn't it? Blame me instead of the reality that some people and situations are not a good fit."

That stung. Meredith took a bracing breath and put her palms down on the cool tabletop. "Let's get back on the subject before we start getting personal, shall we?" *Shall* we? Did she really say that? Suddenly she was a Victorian spinster.

"Fine by me."

"But I want to go on record as saying I don't think you should hire Lenny Doss."

He shrugged. "Then put me on record as saying I still disagree with you on that one."

Big surprise. "Evan, please think about this seriously. The guy is a huge millstone. Obviously Megachannel Network didn't think he was worth the risk, because they let him go."

"I know that," he conceded.

"If you put him on the schedule, and he screws up—as he's *bound* to—it's not just Hanson, it's you, too. You're going to look like a fool. Your reputation will be shot."

He gave a single spike of a laugh. "You can do better than that, Mer. You know I don't care about my reputation."

His use of the old nickname disconcerted her. "Maybe you should."

"Listen," he went on, leaning slightly toward her. "I hear what you're saying, and I promise I took it into consideration before I ever approached Doss. But I really do believe he's learned his lesson. If I thought, as you do, that he was going to be a problem, I wouldn't be trying to hire him. Honestly. Besides, we have a six-second delay in place, too. If he says anything objectionable, it won't make it on air."

"You hope."

"I *know*." He was always good at persuading her away from her better judgment. "Trust me."

Luckily for Meredith, her spine had gotten a

lot stronger in the years since she'd last seen him. "You haven't signed him yet?"

He shook his head. "It's just a matter of time. I'll have an answer in a few days. A week at the most."

"And are you looking into other options in the meantime?'

"Of course."

She nodded, thinking that bought her a little bit of time at least. Now she just needed to get away from this conversation—she needed to get away from *Evan*—so she could pull herself together and figure out a way to solve this problem she found herself swimming in. "Then let's revisit this when you have a better idea of who you're bringing into the company. Once you've hired the talent and set up the schedule, we'll come up with a plan to give you the best possible visibility."

He narrowed his brown eyes slightly and looked at her. "It isn't like you to drop something like this so quickly," he said, his voice tinged with suspicion.

"Maybe it's not like the girl you once knew," she corrected, though he was right. "But you don't know me anymore, Evan."

"So you keep saying."

She sighed. "Look, there's no point in spending the afternoon arguing with you when it's obvious neither one of us is going to back down."

He nodded his agreement.

"And I've got more important things to think about than whether or not you're foolish enough to hire Lenny Doss." She opened her purse, took her wallet out and dropped a bill on the table. "If you'll excuse me now, I'm going back to work." She started to slide out of the booth, not an easy thing to do gracefully, especially when she'd just taken that parting shot.

He looked at the money, then back at her. "I'll pay for lunch, Meredith."

She shook her head. "No need." She stood up and straightened her suit, hoping the gesture would magically bring back the objectivity she seemed to have lost. "Listen, I'm really sorry to have to cut this short, but, like I said, we'll revisit this later." She hoped to God she wouldn't really have to discuss this, or anything else, with him again. "Once you know more about who you're hiring."

"I know who I'm hiring."

"We'll see."

He nodded. "I guess I'll see you around the water cooler."

The old joke, "Not if I see you first," occurred to her, but it wasn't true. The thing that was going to be most difficult about working with Evan was going to be the irresistible urge to be around him.

That was why she had to keep as much distance as she possibly could, starting *now.*

Chapter Five

Meredith stepped out into the hot July sun. Chicago's streets and sidewalks were baking and so was she, but it had less to do with the weather and more to do with being so close to Evan Hanson again.

She'd only stopped a moment to catch her breath when the door opened and he came out behind her. "Oh, good, you're still here," he said.

She whirled to face him. "Evan! Yes, I was just heading back to the office."

He looked her over for a moment then said, simply, "Meredith."

She swallowed. "Yes?"

"Things are a little tense between us."

No sense in being coy about it. "Yes, they are."

"Are you sure you can do this?"

She didn't have to ask what he meant. "Of course. Are you sure *you* can?"

He shrugged. "No problem."

"Good. Why should a little ancient history get in the way of business?" She took a long, deep breath and let it out. "I wasn't expecting to see you today—or any other time, to be perfectly honest with you—and it threw me for a loop." He would never know just how much. "That's all."

"It was a shock for me, too," Evan said. His eyes held a myriad of emotions. "But a good one."

Was he suddenly going sentimental on her? Impossible. She gave a half shrug and nodded. "Then let's have an understanding that from this point on, this is strictly business. Our past, such as it is, has nothing to do with the way we conduct our business. Deal?" She held out her hand.

He took it, sending a surprising tingle up her arm. "Deal." His voice was smooth and low, a man's voice now, yet still horribly familiar. She wondered if she would be able to keep her thoughts of him on a business level.

They held hands for just a fraction of a second longer than they both knew was appropriate. When Evan let go, Meredith's hand felt suddenly cold.

He looked as if he was about to say something but just then his cell phone rang. He took it out of his pocket and glanced at the caller ID. "Damn." He looked at her apologetically. "I've got to take this. Can I get you a cab?"

"No, no. I'm fine. Go back in and take your call."

He flipped his phone open and said to the caller, "Hang on, I'll be right with you," then looked at Meredith. "You're sure? About…everything."

"You bet."

"Okay, I'll be talking to you soon."

"Absolutely."

"Great." He looked at her for a moment. "This will work out just fine." Evan turned to leave. Watching his faded jean-clad form walking away from her, noticing the way his loose-fitting cotton shirt lay across his muscular back and shoulders, Meredith could have sworn she heard him add, "I hope."

The usually short walk back to the office seemed to take forever. With every step the heat got more intense, along with her conflicted feelings.

When she finally got to the building, the air-conditioning hit her like a slap in the face, and she told herself she had to regroup for a moment then make some tough decisions.

She went back to her office. Fortunately David wasn't there—he and his wife, Nina, were taking the kids to the Whistle Stop Circus—so she was alone. Completely alone. She sat down at her desk, a blanket of silence enveloping her like a warm fleece throw.

For a few minutes she couldn't move, couldn't think. All she could do was breathe deeply and try to still her pounding heart. Her eyes burned, but no tears would come, no release.

Just an empty silence.

How had a love that had once been so strong and so comfortable turned into the awkward exchange that had just taken place? It was as if she and Evan were two completely different people now. Strangers.

But they always had been, hadn't they? As it turned out, Evan had never been the person she'd thought he was.

But, darn it, he still looked so much the same. When she'd first laid eyes on him today, her heart had tripped with excitement. Not anger, not sadness, but excitement. Her first impulse was to reach out to him. Then, only after those first split seconds, she remembered why she shouldn't.

Fragmented thoughts of Evan's disappearance, George Hanson's sabotage of her own father's business and her father's subsequent heart attack and death ran through her head. And through it all, Evan had *never* contacted her. He hadn't even sent a card to say he was sorry to hear about her father, and she knew he must have known since it was his father who had had such a strong hand in discrediting her own father's small local newspaper so Hanson's knockoff could take over.

George Hanson had systematically dismantled her father's life. It was child's play for him—just a way to get what he wanted. If Terence Waters wouldn't sell the *Lakeside Gazette* to Hanson—at a greatly undervalued price—then it was the easiest thing in the world for the great George Hanson to force him out of business by creating his own competition.

The *Lake Michigan Gazette*.

The whole business had left her shell-shocked. If Evan had contacted her, said something—*anything*—compassionate, it would have gone a long way toward soothing her shattered nerves.

But he hadn't.

And she'd eventually gotten over him, comfortable in the knowledge that she'd never see him again.

So now that she had, she was paralyzed with a strange combination of resentment and longing.

Gradually the ticking of the wall clock cut into her consciousness, and she managed to stand up and walk to the water cooler. The icy water chilled a path down her throat, returning her senses.

She had to talk to Helen.

She had to tell Helen the truth before this went any further.

Meredith was running on high when she got to Helen's office. She stopped at the desk of Sonia Townsley, Helen's assistant. Sonia was tall, thin, midforties, with striking gray hair cut in a fashionable style that stopped just short of being geometric. But the thing that struck Meredith most about Sonia was that she was always—*always*—calm and cool as a cucumber.

"Is Helen available?" Meredith asked.

"Yes, she is," Sonia said, lowering her perfectly shaped eyebrows. "Are you okay, Meredith?"

Meredith nodded. "I'm fine, really. I just need to talk to Helen for a moment."

"What's going on?" Helen asked from the doorway to her office. She walked out and exchanged concerned looks with Sonia.

"It's just... I..." Meredith stumbled. This was *not* the professional image she sought to project.

"I'll go get some ice water for you," Sonia said, tactfully removing herself from what was clearly an awkward moment.

"I'm sorry," Meredith said to Helen when Sonia had gone. "I didn't mean to drive her away."

"Not at all. Come on in. Tell me what's on your mind." Helen gestured for Meredith to follow her. She sat behind her desk. "Is everything okay?"

Meredith perched uncomfortably on the chair opposite Helen's. "I'm not sure. There's something I think you should know about me. I should have told you before, but I just didn't want to be the sort of person who couldn't separate their personal life from business."

Helen frowned. "But now you find you are?"

"Sort of." Meredith nodded. "I find I could be."

Helen leaned forward. "What is it, Meredith? Tell me what's concerning you and we'll work it out."

"Evan and I have…a past together," Meredith began. She could feel her palms growing clammy and cold.

Helen raised her eyebrows. "Evan?"

"Yes, we knew each other in high school." Understatement. "We knew each other pretty well in high school."

Helen looked over at Meredith with a curious eye. "You're saying you dated?"

Meredith swallowed a lump in her throat. *Dated.* That sounded so impersonal. So milk-shakes-and-a-movie. So innocent. "It was actually a pretty serious relationship. At least it was to me."

"Ah." Helen nodded slowly and leaned back in her chair. "And this is the first time you've seen him since that time?"

"The last time I saw him it was the afternoon of our senior prom. He said he'd see me in a few hours." She gave a dry laugh. "It's been *quite* a few hours."

"I'm sorry, Meredith. It must have been a shock to learn you'd be working with him."

"It was a surprise," Meredith agreed. But, mindful that she didn't want to sound like a whiner who couldn't get over her past, she said, "I'm not saying I can't do what you need me to here—far from it. But my experience with Evan today made me think that, in the interest of full disclosure, I ought to let you know. If you're uncomfortable with me continuing under the circumstances, I'll understand."

Helen smiled. "The circumstances sound like they might lend themselves quite well to your success here. If you already know Evan, already have something of a rapport with him, that might make things easier, don't you think?"

There wasn't going to be anything *easy* about working with Evan, but Meredith nodded. "It could. But it could also make him uncomfortable. If he's reluctant to work with me, I'm not going to be of much use to you."

Helen glanced out the window for a moment with a faraway look in her eyes. Then she turned her attention back to Meredith. "*Is* he reluctant to work with you?"

"I honestly don't know." Meredith gave a self-effacing smile. It would have been too weak for her to admit that she didn't want to work with him. That she was afraid to even be around him. "He didn't seem as rattled by our interaction as I was."

"Are you able to work with him, despite feeling rattled by it?"

This was a moment of truth. Meredith prided herself on her reliability, and this was a turning point in which she could either give in to her weakness and do something she'd probably be ashamed of for the rest of her life or stand tall and work through her discomfort, knowing eventually she'd come out on the other side of it.

Intellectually, it was an easy choice.

"Yes," she said, more comfortable following her intellect than her heart.

"Then let's leave things as they are," Helen said, locking eyes with Meredith. "You came highly recommended, and with everything the company has been through recently we need the best people we can get so that Hanson Media Group recovers its once stellar reputation."

"I'll do my best." Meredith stood to go. She was feeling a little bit better now and was embarrassed about the alarmist manner in which she'd come to Helen at first. "I'm just glad you know the truth now."

"I am, too," Helen said. "Thank you."

Meredith left the office, then stopped outside the closed door and took a deep breath. She couldn't tell Helen *everything,* of course, but she'd at least told her what she needed to know about Meredith's past. Hopefully now that wouldn't come back to bite her.

Meredith set off down the hall, looking for David, when she ran straight into Evan.

He looked at her, then looked behind her at Helen's office door.

"Meeting with the boss?"

She swallowed. "One of them."

"Anything I should know about?"

She took a short breath. "No. Nothing important."

He looked at her for one long, hard moment. Then, without a word, he turned and walked away.

Chapter Six

Helen arrived at Shabu Hachi two minutes early for her 8:00 p.m. meeting with Ichiro Kobayashi, of the media conglomerate TAKA Corporation.

The restaurant hostess led Helen to the table where Ichiro Kobayashi and another man waited for her.

She smiled and bowed slightly, holding out a business card bearing her information in both English and Japanese to Kobayashi. He handed her one in return, likewise in English and Japanese, and though his manner was nothing short of courteous, she had the distinct sense that he was unhappy at having to deal with a woman instead of a man.

She repeated the process with the other man and felt the same sense of disconcertion from him.

His card said he was Chion Kinjo and he worked in acquisitions for TAKA, along with Kobayashi. His card listed offices in Tokyo, Kyoto and Shizuoka.

TAKA was a huge corporation.

It was distinctly possible that Helen was in over her head. She just needed to make sure she didn't let on that she felt that way.

She put the cards in her pocket, then took out a small ornament she'd purchased from a Chicago artisan and gave it to Kobayashi as a souvenir of Chicago. It was customary, but she also hoped he would keep it and be reminded that this was a town he liked and wanted to return to.

"This is for you," she said. "It's a token of thanks and, I hope, a happy reminder of our beautiful city."

He turned it in his hand and gave a nod of approval. "Very lovely. The detail is magnificent."

Helen breathed one small sigh of relief. So far, so good, given the fact that they would rather have been dealing with her late husband than with her.

Kobayashi indicated she should sit next to him,

which she took as a good sign. The moment they were seated, a waitress brought water to the table and, after a brief exchange with Kinjo in Japanese, filled their glasses, bowed and left the table.

"I've taken the liberty of suggesting a variety of foods from the eastern region of our country," Kobayashi said to Helen. "I hope that's agreeable to you?"

"Indeed." Helen nodded. "It's not often one gets to take a culinary tour like this with a native. I look forward to trying your selections."

This seemed to please Kobayashi. He gave a polite smile then leaped right into business. "I'm sorry to hear of your husband's death," he said. "I would have liked to have met him."

Had George been alive, there was no way he would have considered talking to these men about a merger. He would sooner have driven the company into bankruptcy.

In fact, he all but had.

"He was a good man," she said, swallowing the lie as smoothly as a tall glass of lemonade.

"As far as his company is concerned, my associate and I have grave concerns about the recent performance of Hanson Media."

Helen nodded. "I understand. However, a

comparative study would show that American media companies are all undergoing growing pains right now."

"Growing pains?" he repeated.

Shoot, she'd meant to avoid idioms. "Difficulty in a changing market," she explained. "Culturally speaking, things are changing rapidly in the United States, and a lot of news outfits have been hit hard trying to strike a balance between news, information and entertainment."

"Does that not make this a risky investment?"

"No, that makes this a savvy investment." Helen steeled her nerve. It was going to take a lot of confidence for her to pull this one off. "The reason for the growing pains in the media industry is that the growth is so rapid. Any investment made today will be multiplied tenfold within just a few years."

"Then why are you selling interest in the company?" Kinjo asked shrewdly.

She leveled her gaze on him. "Because I want Hanson Media Group to be heard around the world—" she cocked her head "—and I believe you want the same for TAKA. Together, Hanson and TAKA would be a very, *very* powerful force in world media."

The two men maintained masks of impassive

consideration. Not one readable emotion so much as flickered across either one of their faces.

"You wish to maintain some control over Hanson Media Group?" Kobayashi asked.

Helen turned her gaze to him and leveled it. "I'm looking for a merger, Mr. Kobayashi, not a takeover."

The men exchanged glances.

"We are not in need of saving," Helen added, although it was as preposterous as a drowning victim trying to negotiate with a lifeguard before accepting help. "We are in *want* of power. We believe that with TAKA we can achieve that. For both our companies."

"TAKA is already powerful," Kobayashi said in a clipped voice. "It is my impression that that is why you approached us with this offer."

She wanted to point out that it was a *proposal* more than an *offer.* Characterizing it as an offer made it sound as if she were willing to sacrifice Hanson Media Group completely, and she wasn't.

But Helen knew it didn't make sense to argue with the man, particularly since Kobayashi wasn't the person ultimately making the decision. Better to play nice and try and work up their interest. "TAKA could be *more* powerful," she said, smiling confidently.

Kobayashi didn't answer that directly, but the short breath he took before speaking again gave him away. He wasn't willing to walk away.

He was at least interested.

"There is one concern we have, which you have not addressed," he said to her.

"What's that?" Apprehension nibbled at Helen's nerves. Were they going to throw a curve ball her way?

"Hanson Media Group appears to have a growing liability in the radio division. We believe this is endangering any investment advantages."

The radio division was turning out to be more trouble than Helen had anticipated. But after all the time she had spent longing for more contact with George's children, she wasn't about to offer one of them the opportunity to help the company then snatch it away.

Besides, she had faith in Evan. He didn't have a lot of nine-to-five business experience, but he was smart as a whip. And he had a good sense of what people in their company's most desirable demographic wanted.

"I've just hired new staff to head the radio division, including my late husband's son, Evan."

She smiled, hoping her confidence in Evan shone through, rather than the occasional uncertainty she felt as George Hanson's widow.

"It is our understanding that he is intending to change your programming to what you call 'shock jock' programs, specifically that of a Len Doss, who has already cost other broadcasting companies hundreds of thousands of dollars in Federal Communications Commission fines."

Helen was surprised that Kobayashi had this information, which should've been classified. But she trusted Evan and Meredith to do what was best for the company.

"Hanson Broadcasting hasn't made any commitments to Mr. Doss. It is Evan's full intention to investigate the possibility thoroughly and make an educated decision based on the balance of risks and gains." She gave her brightest smile. "And if Evan Hanson decides that hiring Mr. Doss is in the company's best interest, I have absolute faith in him."

"Is that so?"

She nodded, and she meant it. Evan knew what appealed to young men his age more than she or Kobayashi did, that she was certain of. "Believe me, the division is in excellent hands."

Kobayashi looked dubious. "Are you able to prove that?"

"Our numbers for the next quarter should bear it out." She took a steadying breath. "Believe me, Mr. Kobayashi, *nothing* is standing in the way of Hanson Media and nationwide success."

Spying was such an ugly word.

Meredith preferred to think of herself as brokering information that would benefit all parties involved.

She was an *investigator,* not a corporate spy.

Still, as she crept around the offices of Hanson Media Group by the fluorescent semi-light of 2:30 a.m., jumping at every tiny noise, she felt like a spy. A sneak.

A liar.

Yes, she was doing what her employer had hired her to do. This was, in reality, her job. And she'd do it well; she always did. But this time it was personal, and that made all the difference. Instead of gathering sensitive corporate information from one company and handing it over to another, she was gathering sensitive information about Hanson Media—a name that had invoked various strong and conflicted feelings in her for over a decade—and providing it to a company that potentially wanted to take over and push the Hansons out entirely.

Meredith didn't know what her employer's ultimate goal for the company was: it wasn't her job to know.

It was her job to collect pertinent information and pass it along to her boss.

The ignorance of what would then happen because of it should have been bliss.

She wouldn't let her trepidation stop her, though. It was just raw emotion, and this job had no room for emotion. Emotion was a liar. It made a person believe things that might not be true. Whatever she felt, she needed to soldier on and get the job done.

Just as she'd always done.

So she proceeded. Her heart pounded with the fear that someone—some weary soul who wanted to get his work done before taking his family to Disney World, or some ambitious soul who wanted to impress his boss with work done early—would show up around one of the quiet corners.

But the only sound was the hum of the building air conditioner, whooshing cold air through miles of air ducts.

Meredith went to David Hanson's office first.

With any luck she'd find everything she needed there and she wouldn't have to dig around in anyone else's files.

With a quick glance to make sure no one was standing in the shadows watching her, she turned on his computer to look for the files he'd told her about earlier in the week.

"You can see our recent performance history broken down by day, week, month and year," he'd said, proud of a former administrative assistant's elaborate spreadsheets. "It's like forensic science. I can tell you how many newspapers were sold in lower Manhattan by 1:00 p.m. on Tuesday, January 13. I can tell you how many people listened to Garrett Pinchon's Gospel Hour every Sunday morning from 1998 to last November."

This was just the kind of information her boss wanted to look at.

When the operating system on David's computer came up, she typed in the password she'd watched him enter earlier.

Bubby.

Whatever that meant.

The system beeped and rattled through the rest of its processes and produced a desktop background photo of David's wife, Nina, and his

kids—Zach and Izzy, he'd told her proudly—
smiling at the camera and giving Meredith a
twinge of guilt.

Pushing the negative thoughts away, Meredith
quickly maneuvered her way through the system,
finding the files David had alluded to earlier. She
zipped them into a single file, then saved them to
a thumb drive she'd put into a USB port. Once
upon a time this had been the stuff of CIA espionage. Nowadays, every college student in North
America could carry the equivalent of every
paper they'd written since elementary school on
a device no bigger than a child's thumb.

It worked for Meredith, who was currently
saving spreadsheets that would have sucked up
all the memory and then some on an older
computer. Even now it wasn't an instantaneous
process. She tapped her fingers impatiently on
the desktop while the large files took their time
being converted and transferred.

At one point Meredith thought she heard a
sound like a cough in the distance. Immediately
her hand flew to the monitor button, and she
turned it off, waiting breathlessly in the dark to
see if a security guard or, worse, another employee would come to investigate the quiet hum
of David's hard drive as it did her bidding.

She waited a good five minutes in the dark, holding her breath nearly the entire time. Finally, thinking it must have been her imagination, she crept to the door and peered around the corner, down the hall. She braced herself for a shock.

Nothing.

With a sigh of profound relief, she went back to David's office. The computer had finished saving. She pocketed the thumb drive, erased her virtual footsteps on the system and shut the computer down.

Still cautious, she listened with the paranoid awareness of a lone wolf at night as she made her way through the maze of halls.

She saw no one. Heard no one. But she had the most disquieting feeling that someone else was there. Maybe it was surveillance cameras. Or building security out in the main hall. Or the constant hum of countless computers hibernating or showing *Star Wars* screensavers to no one.

For one crazy instant Meredith thought about going to Evan's office. Something about the still of the night and some long-dormant knot of emotions called her there. As if she could go and breathe him in…and breathe him out. And maybe get rid of the memories that haunted her still, once and for all.

But there was no time for that. She'd done what she needed to do and now she needed to get the heck out of the building before anyone figured her out.

She opened the main door and, after a surreptitious glance out into the hallway, she stepped away, letting the door to Hanson Media Group close harder than she'd intended.

It was a careless mistake, but it didn't matter. She'd proven to herself time and again that there was no one there.

No one but the ghosts of a man who once meant the world to her and whose name now meant only a biweekly paycheck, excellent health and dental insurance and a dull ache in her heart that she almost couldn't bear.

Chapter Seven

Evan Hanson woke to a bang.

He sat bolt upright in the converted sofa bed before he had even a moment to think, his body tensed and ready for fight or flight. For one crazy, disconcerting moment he couldn't remember where he was, then it came back to him. He was sleeping in his office. Unable to commit to staying in Chicago—or even admit to himself that he'd come back—he'd been camping out in the office, using the executive washroom for bathing and either eating out or ordering food in.

What point would there be in getting an

apartment to keep a job that he knew wasn't going to last long? He was no ace executive but he could see the writing on the wall—Hanson Media Group was going down. If he could do anything to help stop it, he was willing to give it a hundred percent, but at the same time he wasn't going to bet his life that it would work out. Not that he wanted to come out and say that to anyone still working there.

Either way, there was no way he was going to be in Chicago for the rest of his life.

He missed the sun of Majorca. The fresh regional produce he'd come to enjoy picking up at sunny outdoor markets across Europe. Already he felt like one more quickie takeout meal would kill him.

Helen's hopes for the company were admirable. Noble, even. But impossible. Anyone could see that. Offices that used to be filled with enthusiastic employees, reflecting the prosperity of what was once one of the most powerful media groups in the United States, were now half empty. There was little laughter, less water cooler talk, and almost no optimism on the faces of the employees he saw every day.

Most of Hanson's best employees had left a while back, knowing their résumés would look better if they reflected tenure at a successful company than if they showed a tenacious grip on a ship that was going down faster than the *Titanic*. It might not stay down—he was fairly sure some other company would snatch it up at a bargain price—but it was going to go down long enough for those onboard to suffer. Unless they were brave enough to hold on to their stock options until the price went up.

But from what he was hearing around the office, most people weren't. The general consensus was "get out while you can."

So what the heck was Meredith Waters doing here?

The Meredith he'd known was far too savvy to align herself with a losing cause.

And honestly, it would have suited him a whole lot better not to have her around. She was a distraction.

A *major* distraction.

Hell, Meredith's ghost had haunted him for years, her memory floating around the outskirts of his consciousness more frequently than he liked to admit. He didn't always see it, but often, late at night, when it was just him and his thoughts alone in a room, it was Meredith's voice that spoke to him.

Which was nuts, because he knew she had to hate him by then. He knew that she wasn't lying in another bed across the ocean, thinking the same thoughts. And he was fairly certain that she had moved on to a much better and more reliable prospect.

Someone he could never live up to.

He'd spent a lifetime feeling as though he couldn't live up to his loved ones' expectations. For a long time it was his failure in his father's eyes that had disturbed him the most. One would have thought after the snub in the reading of the will that his feeling of failure toward his father would have grown even deeper, but something in him had snapped. Somehow—by some miracle—he had stopped caring what his father thought.

And for a brief but glorious time he'd enjoyed the feeling of not caring what *anyone* thought.

Then Meredith had appeared. And suddenly who he was as a man, and what she thought of him, mattered more than ever.

And *that* was what was distracting him the most. It was going to be hard to get her out of his mind: he knew that the moment he first saw her.

He had spent his life since Meredith dating a series of women who were ill-suited for him. He preferred it that way. A fling was one thing, but he'd felt love before and he didn't ever want to feel it again. And he'd definitely avoided anyone who reminded him at all of Meredith. It was too painful.

At first it was a conscious effort, but soon it had become a habit. He dated blondes. He dated redheads. Deep black hair was fine.

But he never dated girls with that rich, chestnut-colored hair, or pale Irish skin, or laughing green eyes.

He thought of her, and how she had always applied herself completely to every task, whether it was studying for a history exam or helping a friend fill out a college application, or simply making that amazing sour-cream bread she used to make.

He doubted any of the women he had dated in the past decade could make their own breakfast, much less their own bread.

But he couldn't afford to make those comparisons now, or think of the things he had once loved about Meredith. Particularly now, when they were laboring through this frigid situation they had found themselves in.

Yet even while part of him resisted their new business relationship, he knew she would do the job well. He knew if anyone could help him succeed, it would be Meredith.

And they'd agreed that that was what they were going to do. They were going to work together and make the business succeed. Regardless of what had happened or not happened between them in the past.

The past was dead.

The future was short, at least here at Hanson Media.

All he needed to do was whatever he could to bring about the success of the radio division, then he could get the hell out of Chicago.

His thoughts returned to Lenny Doss. Sure, the guy was a bit of a renegade. He was definitely notorious. But Evan had faith that Lenny could keep his nose clean as far as the FCC regulations went. Lenny was brash, Lenny was bold, Lenny was crude, but Lenny was not stupid.

And he was popular.

Unable to sleep, Evan went to his desk and booted up his computer to check his e-mail. That seemed to be Lenny's preferred method of communication, so Evan decided he'd write to the guy and ask if he'd made a decision about the contract Evan had offered him.

Amidst what looked like a hundred spam messages offering everything from investment opportunities to physical enhancement, Evan found an e-mail from Lenny himself.

To: ehanson@hansonmediagroup.com
From: ossmanhimself@lennydoss.com
Subject: You've got competition, Bud!

Yo man! DigiDog Satellite Radio has given me a pretty sweet offer. You willing to up yours by 10% with a three-year guarantee? That's the only way you'll get the Doss Man.
LD

Evan muttered an oath.

He quickly typed DigiDog into a search engine. It turned out they were an up-and-coming satellite company and they were paying big bucks to acquire high-profile talent—which could certainly define Lenny Doss—as well as high-end music catalogs. A quick scan of the projected programming showed that DigiDog had expended a lot of money already on what was really an uncertain venture.

Lenny Doss's name, however, did not come up in a search of DigiDog. Not even in tangentially related articles in which programming directors talked about their dream lineups. So the question of whether anyone had actually approached Lenny Doss with a deal wasn't necessarily answered. They *might* have, but then again, it could have been a ploy on Lenny's part to work up Hanson Media's enthusiasm for him.

The problem was that Evan couldn't be sure which it was. And Evan was convinced that Lenny Doss was the first and most important step toward success for Hanson Broadcasting. He was sure of it.

After just several minutes' consideration, he came up with a plan.

"I'm taking Lenny Doss out for drinks tonight and you need to come with us and convince him to sign on with Hanson," Evan said to Meredith later that morning.

What he didn't say was *please,* though the word repeated itself in his mind.

"*What?* You're joking, right?"

"Nope. Dominick's on Navy Pier. Seven-thirty or so." He could already picture her there, in the soft light of Dominick's, wearing something—anything—other than her conservative work clothes.

"And you want me to come with you," she said incredulously, watching his brown eyes for signs that he was just pulling her leg. Especially given the heated conversation they'd already had about the wisdom of hiring Lenny Doss.

"Yes, I do," Evan said, straight-faced. She could always tell when he was joking, because even though he could keep his mouth still he always got a hint of a dimple on the left side. She used to think it was adorable.

There was no dimple now.

He wasn't kidding.

"Why would I do that, Evan?" she asked. "Why would I go out and actively try to hire a guy like that?"

"Because you know I want to bring him on board."

"And you know I'm adamantly against it."

"And you know you're wrong about that."

"I do not!"

"Well, I do." He took her by the arm and led her to his office, saying, "Technically, I'm your boss and you need to do what I ask you to."

She wrenched free of his grasp and said, "Yeah, well, technically, I'm not working for your department, so you have to clear this kind of thing with your stepmother, and I think if she reviewed both sides of this issue, she'd be inclined to agree with me."

"Not if she looked at the facts."

"What facts could possibly condone what he's done?" Meredith wanted to know.

Evan stopped walking and looked at her. "Nothing can *condone* what he's done, but his statistics are impressive and that makes him worth considering, even if you don't like his past."

"It's his future I'm concerned with."

They rounded the corner into Evan's office and he said, "That's why you need to consider *all* the facts, not just the Internet gossip you've looked up."

She shot him a look of disagreement, but he was right. She'd known as soon as he'd mentioned Lenny Doss's name that the guy was a ticking time bomb, so she'd gone online looking for evidence that proved her right, not evidence that proved her wrong.

Apparently Evan had done the opposite.

As usual.

"You've got to look at the statistics here." He sat her down in his chair and leaned across her to type an Internet address into his computer. "Check out the numbers on WRFK," he said, pointing at a chart on the computer screen. "This is about the time they moved from a regular news format to talk radio with Lenny Doss."

Meredith leaned forward and looked, taking the mouse in hand and moving around the chart a bit to get a more detailed picture. "What month did they hire him?" she asked, concentrating on the demographics and the charted increase in listeners.

"February." He pointed. "Right there."

"Mmm-hmm." She clicked on the date and checked for the entire programming schedule, to see if there was another reason that could account for all or some of the increase. "They also had religious programming on Sundays at that time," she pointed out half-heartedly. Religious programming virtually never pulled in big ratings.

"Check the ratings," Evan said, his voice ringing with smug confidence at what she'd find.

She checked. The religious programming had abysmal ratings. Worse than most. "Oh."

"Exactly."

Meredith frowned, looking for any evidence there might be that Evan was assigning too much credit to this one man. "When did they fire him?"

"They didn't."

"No?" Darn it, she should have armed herself with more specific information before meeting with Evan about this.

"He left for Gemini Broadcasting here." He pointed at the computer screen again, leaning so close across Meredith that she could smell not only his cologne but the achingly familiar scent of his skin. "In November of the following year."

"And the ratings went down," Meredith observed, so distracted by the close proximity of Evan that she almost couldn't concentrate on the matter at hand.

Evan, on the other hand, didn't appear to be having any such problem being close to Meredith. He gave a chipper nod, his face devoid of anything other than triumph that Meredith appeared to be seeing the light, now that he was shining it directly in her eyes. "The ratings went way down."

She went back to the search engine and typed in Gemini Broadcasting, just as Evan had a week earlier, and typed in the pertinent dates.

He waited a moment while she studied the higher ratings before saying, "See what I mean?"

She clicked off and rolled back in the chair to face him. "Yes, I do."

"But you're conflicted because, while you like what he could potentially do for the company, you don't like what he stands for," Evan said, trying to read the unaccustomed sternness in her eyes and her posture. Every time he got anywhere near her she tensed up and resisted whatever he was saying.

If she'd shown any form of emotion at all—which she hadn't—he'd have thought her reaction to him was personal.

As it was, he could only conclude that she hated Lenny Doss, or what he stood for, so much that she felt angry at Evan for even wanting to hire him and for pointing out that there were good things to be considered in the process.

"Right," she admitted, taking a short breath and moving slightly away from where Evan stood. The chair she was sitting in knocked against the desk behind her. "But as I've said before, I'm also hesitant about his potential as a liability. That's really important," she added.

"Fine. Check the e-mails he's written to me about that," Evan said, switching to another program and pulling up a folder in which he'd stored his correspondence with Lenny Doss. He kept a little more distance this time, not so much because he was afraid to get near her because of her reaction, but because he didn't want to see her react by recoiling again.

If she did, he'd know it was on purpose and not just some small coincidence, and he didn't want to know that. "Read them all, if it will make you feel better," he said, stepping back and going to the small refrigerator under the picture window to take out a bottle of spring water and give himself something to do other than just stand there gazing at Meredith and trying to figure out how the years had only made her prettier instead of older.

"Okay." She looked back at the screen. "Just give me a couple of minutes."

He hadn't thought she'd really do that, but it was nice to be away from her scrutiny for a moment, even though it seemed like forever that he stood there waiting for her to read through the e-mails.

One by one, date by date, she clicked through, stopping every once in a while to make a note on the small pad on his desk.

He noticed that her handwriting was still the same messy scrawl it had been in high school. Something about that small fact made him feel a little warmer inside.

A little more at home.

But that was all she gave in terms of comforting vibes. The rest of her was completely cool and impersonal. He tried to read the expression on her face, but though the face itself was undeniably familiar, some of the expressions she wore now were completely new to him. He had only his experience with people to go by, and he got the distinct and uncomfortable feeling that, for Meredith, this was all just standard business.

Finally she finished scrolling through the notes and turned the chair around to face Evan. Her green eyes were bright, probably from the sudden light change of looking from the computer monitor to Evan, and she said, "Okay, I will admit I *kind of* see your point."

He couldn't believe his ears. "You *agree* with me?"

"Wait a minute." She held up a slender hand. The left one, actually.

The one he'd once thought would wear his wedding and engagement rings.

"I didn't say I *agree* with you," she went on, blissfully ignorant of his disconcerting thoughts about their past. "There's still plenty we disagree about."

That hadn't always been the case.

"But I am saying," she continued, "that I see your point about his ratings and I understand why his contrition has given you confidence in potentially hiring him."

This was good. She was agreeing with him. Wasn't she? "So you'll come with me and meet him?"

She frowned, hesitating. Her delicate brow lowered toward those bright green eyes in a way that he hadn't seen in so long it made him ache to think about it.

"I'm not sure there's anything *I* could do to help you attain your goal."

"Come on, Mer," he said, catching the familiarity only afterward, when it was too late to stop himself. "You can charm the pants off him, that's what you can do. You're damn good at that."

She glanced at him sharply and said, "I don't think any of us wants that."

He had to be careful of this thinking about her personally, because obviously some part of his subconscious was having trouble distinguishing between the way he used to feel about her, back when they were just kids, versus what he felt for her now that they were nothing more than casual work associates.

What he needed to concentrate on was the success of his plan. Securing Lenny Doss and saving the company. The idea had taken hold and was mattering more and more to him. He couldn't say for sure if his desire was more a compulsion to help future generations who were innocent of his father's poison, or if he just wanted to "show up" the old man by saving the company that George had nearly destroyed.

He wanted both, but the balance tended to swing a little more toward the latter than the former.

Not that it mattered. Everyone involved had a common goal, and it didn't matter how they got there, did it?

"Okay, I'm sorry," he said. "But you know what I mean. There's a lot you can do to help persuade him, because you are a smart, beautiful wo—person. And you can present the case in a truthful and persuasive manner."

She faced him, looking surprised for a moment, then gave one conciliatory nod. "Your faith in me might be a little unfounded. But, fine, I'll do it."

"You'll go?" He couldn't believe it.

It was almost a date.

At least, the prospect of it made him feel as nervous as he would have if it was a first date. And he was seventeen.

"I'll go." She nodded again, that rich brown hair gleaming in the light. "But only to meet the guy and feel the situation out. I'm not promising I'm going to be buying a ticket for the Lenny Doss love train."

"Honey, that train doesn't even stop at this station," Evan said with a smile. He could have pulled her into his arms and kissed her at that moment, but he didn't.

This was business, he reminded himself. And everything that happened would remain just business, even if the look in her eyes or the curve of her mouth made him think of things that were distinctly unbusinesslike.

So he would take on the manner of the gregarious boss, enthusiastic about his work. "All we need to be concerned with is the Lenny Doss ratings train. And that—" he opened his arms "—is about to call Hanson Broadcasting its home station."

Chapter Eight

This was, of course, *not* a date. And they both knew it. So Meredith hated the impulse she had to make herself up for the evening.

More than that, she hated that she wasn't able to stop feeling the impulse.

Her mother had moved back to Tampa almost a year ago now, and Meredith was back in the suburban Chicago home she'd grown up in. It had made sense for her to move in, since her mother wasn't emotionally ready to let go of the house, yet wasn't physically able to maintain it any longer.

Meredith was back in Chicago for her work and, since she needed a place to live, the old house had fit the bill perfectly, though it was sometimes disconcerting to find herself having her Cheerios in the same old kitchen.

That was changing. Meredith wasn't the sort of person who could actually live in that kind of time warp. But renovation was going slowly, thanks in part to slow contractors and in part to Meredith's limited funds, so the house still looked very much as it had ten or twenty years ago.

This hadn't bothered her at all until now, when she was looking into a bathroom mirror that had reflected her image when it was that of a fresh-faced high-school girl getting ready for a date with the somewhat wild, but deep-down sweet, bad boy Evan Hanson himself.

"You shouldn't be going out with that kid," her father had told her one night as she was getting ready to go see the new Hal Burkett movie with Evan. "He comes from a bad family."

"Oh, Daddy, he doesn't come from a bad family. His father's just a bully, that's all."

Her father had snorted and it was only now that she understood the pain that had tightened his expression for a moment. "If the boy is anything like his father, you would do best to stay as far away from him as possible."

"He's really great, Daddy. Honest. You trust my judgment, don't you?"

"I don't trust anything where George Hanson's family is concerned."

She'd gone to him and hugged him tight, her arms closing too easily around a frame that used to have a lot more bulk to it. He wasn't healthy. He worked all the time. She worried about that.

"Evan must have had a wonderful mother, because he's one of the best guys I ever met. Besides you, of course. I know she's gone now, but he had her up until last year. That's a lot of time for him to learn to be something other than his father."

"You always see the best in people," her father had said with something like amazement. "But you have to believe me when I tell you that sometimes people are not what they seem. Trust, but always be at least a little cautious. Take care of yourself when I'm not there to do it for you."

She'd kissed his cheek. "I'll be fine, Daddy, I promise you."

Her own words had echoed tauntingly in her memory for some time after that.

Now look at her.

Life had changed a lot since those days, yet here Meredith was, still looking at the same old face—though somewhat older—in the same old mirror, trying to accent the same old green eyes and too-full lips to make the same old boy think she was pretty.

She had to be crazy.

Why did this matter so much to her?

It didn't, she told herself as she carefully brushed a mossy green shadow in a thin line along her lashes. Not too much, just enough to make her eyes stand out.

It made sense that she should look her best for a meeting with talent the company was trying to hire, didn't it?

So this wasn't really to impress Evan, she reminded herself as she struggled to bring her long, wavy, chestnut-colored hair under control with a ceramic flat iron. She merely wanted to look her best so that these men would take her seriously *professionally.* It would have been foolish for her to face them with the distraction of sleep-deprived pale skin and wild, unruly hair.

She had to make herself look like the sleek professional she was.

The clock ticked slowly forward as she

prepared for the evening. The truth was, the time seemed to be going extra slowly. It didn't take that long to do her makeup and hair, but she was so agitated about spending the evening out with Evan that she wanted to keep busy until it was time to leave.

Instead, she found herself dressed up with nowhere to go and nothing to think about other than Evan for an hour before she needed to leave for Navy Pier.

Meredith purposely waited in her car an extra few minutes before meeting Evan and Lenny Doss.

Evan had volunteered to pick her up and give her a ride, but she had declined, and though she couldn't say exactly why, it probably had a lot to do with the fact that it was weird enough seeing Evan again—she couldn't quite bring herself to look at him under the front porch light of her parents' house right now. It would be just too…eerie.

Besides, she wanted to maintain as much control over the situation as she could. And as she sat in the car watching the minutes tick away on the digital readout in the dash, she reminded herself that was exactly what she was doing.

Maintaining control.

Ten minutes past the time that her stomach began twisting and telling her to hurry up you can't be late she got out of her car, pushed the lock button on her key chain and walked at a measured pace to the restaurant.

Her biggest dread was being the first one there, sitting like an idiot alone at the table waiting for a man she had once known and loved.

Fortunately, both men in question were already there, sitting at a mercifully large round table with half-filled glasses of beer in front of them.

Evan looked amazing in a light-blue band collar cotton shirt and khakis that emphasized his physique without being so tight they looked like he was about to hit the dance floor for a disco contest.

Lenny, on the other hand, was wearing exactly that kind of pants: tight dark-blue jeans with a loud Hawaiian-print shirt that looked about two sizes too small and should have had at least three more buttons fastened in order to look acceptable, if not great.

"Meredith," Evan called when he saw her. He stood up and beckoned her over to the chair next to him.

Was it her imagination or did he looked relieved?

Meredith gave a smile of thanks to the hostess, took a short, bracing breath and smiled at the two men. "Hi there. I'm sorry if I'm late."

"Not at all," Evan said. "Please, sit down. This is Lenny Doss. Lenny, this is Meredith Waters. She works in the publicity department. She'll be helping us come up with some promotional ideas for your return to network broadcasting."

"Oh?" She shot Evan a questioning glance. "Did the two of you come to terms on a contract?"

"Not yet," Lenny said. "But now that I get a gander at the talent they got back at the office, I gotta say, I'm a little more inclined to sign."

Evan's ire was immediately up. "Hey—"

Meredith put a hand up to stop him. She could handle this herself, without ugliness. "It's the on-air talent that we're concerned with at the moment, Mr. Doss. Do you think you can really live up to our expectations?"

Lenny started posturing, exactly as she'd thought he would. "Just you watch," he said, sliding a hand through his slicked-back, thinning hair.

The waitress stopped by and discreetly took Meredith's order for a glass of Chardonnay.

"And can you keep yourself in line?" Meredith went on to Lenny. "It's my understanding that you've had a little trouble with that in the past. Hanson Media won't put up with you incurring FCC fines, you know."

"It's in the contract," Evan said to her quietly.

She was impressed. For a guy who'd never really worked in the business world, he was pretty good. She turned and gave him a quick wink.

"So what about it, Mr. Doss?" she asked, then took a sip of her wine. It was bitter. She hated wine, actually, but not as much as she hated beer or any of the other alternatives. And ordering a soda would have looked so prim and proper that a guy like this would probably have held it against her. "Should we give you a chance? And if so, why?"

He wasn't that easy, unfortunately. "The question is, should *I* give *you* a chance." He took a long swig of his beer then belched hideously. The look in his eyes was one of sheer pride. "And I'm not so sure about that yet."

Evan moved in his chair, effectively putting himself fractionally closer to Meredith. He didn't do it consciously, she could tell, but it was a protective move nevertheless.

And she found it comforting.

She sank, ever so slightly, against his presence and, bolstered by that, said to Lenny, "You're going to have to make up your mind, because we're in talks with Howard Stern, as well."

Lenny's eyes shot up to hers. "You are?" Then he frowned and said, "No way. No, you aren't."

"He costs more than you do," she said casually, taking a roll out of the basket in the center of the table. "But, as you know, he's got better ratings."

"Only because he's been in more markets."

She shrugged and pulled the roll apart, buttering half of it with deliberate slowness. "I don't know. We're just looking at the bottom line. Right, Evan?"

His brown eyes were bright with amusement. It looked as if he'd been planning to simply sit back and watch the conversation between Lenny and Meredith unfold, so when she mentioned his name it took a second for him to say, "Right. Bottom line. It's all about the bottom line."

Lenny's small dark eyes shot from Meredith to Evan and back again. She could practically see his mind working. "I hear that," he said, with much forced casualness. "Uh-huh." His cell phone rang—an aggressive measure from a Green Day song—and he pulled it out of his pocket and flipped it open. "Yo," he said into the phone. "Speak."

After a moment, he said, "Heeyyyy, Roberts." Meredith guessed by "Roberts" he was talking about Karl Roberts, his agent. "I'm just meeting here with Hanson and a chick from the publicity department. They're trying to talk me into signing but I don't know, man. What you got for me? Is Clear Channel Radio still nipping at us, too?" He flashed a self-satisfied glance at Evan and Meredith.

It disappeared quickly, though. "What's that?" Lenny asked. It may have been Meredith's imagination, but she thought she saw panic flicker in Lenny's eyes. "They're not?" He glanced in Evan's direction again and quickly turned away, saying, "So what's their offer?"

Another pause during which Lenny looked distinctly uncomfortable. "Interesting. But I want to wait and see what Hanson can come up with. It's not just about the money. I like these guys." He winked at Evan and Meredith. "You tell Clear Channel they're just going to have wait and see what I do with Hanson. I think they may pull through with the winning bid." He smiled, but his face had definitely paled a shade or two.

Meredith took the opportunity to turn to Evan and when she did she saw by the telltale dimple that he was holding back a smile. So he was clearly hearing everything she was, and they both knew they had Lenny Doss in their sights if they wanted him.

"All right, man," Lenny said, paling another shade. "There's more to a deal than just money. You let me finish talking to Hanson here and I'll give you a call back. In the meantime, you can tell Clear Channel to just cool their jets. We'll answer them when we're ready." He flipped the phone shut and put it back in his pocket, shaking his head and muttering, "Agents. Can't live with them, can't kill them."

Meredith smiled. "Was that your agent?" She knew it was, of course, and she was almost positive from all of Lenny's blustering and body language that Hanson was his only offer. She almost felt sorry for him.

Nevertheless, she had to play hardball.

Lenny nodded in answer to her question. He was clearly trying to appear ultracasual. "Yeah, he's going on about some other offer. But, as you may have heard, I'm interested in what Hanson's putting out there."

"You know what Hanson's putting out there," Evan said, then made a point of looking at his watch. "But listen, Len, I've got time constraints tonight, and I know Meredith is on her way someplace else, so I think we're going to have to wrap this up."

Meredith nodded, picking up Evan's cue. "That's right." She glanced at Evan. "Don't you have an appointment tomorrow to speak with...?" She mumbled a name that she hoped sounded like Artie Petro, one of Lenny's biggest competitors.

Evan picked right up on it. "Yes, I do."

They both turned to Lenny, who now looked like a raccoon caught going through the trash in the middle of the night.

"Then let's sign, man," he said loudly. "Let's get this show on the road."

"Okay, then." Evan smiled. "We'll get the contracts to your agent tomorrow."

"Great. Got another appointment," Lenny said. "This one's personal, if you know what I mean." He gave Evan a lascivious wink.

"I know *exactly* what you mean," Evan told him evenly, his voice hard but tinged with humor.

Meredith had to suppress a giggle.

Lenny nodded, oblivious. "Monday morning, 6:00 a.m. shift?"

"You've got it," Evan said.

Meredith was amazed at how soon Evan had him slated to start, but she said nothing.

"Great." Lenny gave a bobbing nod. "So, it was cool meeting you," he said to Meredith. "Evan, man, I look forward to working with you."

"Same here," Evan said. "You just make sure you keep yourself in line. Don't forget paragraph eleven."

Lenny looked blank. "Paragraph eleven?"

Evan nodded. "The contract you're about to sign. Paragraph eleven says you pay all FCC fines you incur and that incurring such a fine makes our side of the contract null and void."

"Oh, that." Lenny waved a hand, but there was a nervousness in his eyes that he couldn't hide. "Don't worry about a thing," he assured them. "I'll be walking the straight and narrow. No problem."

"You're sure?" Meredith interjected worriedly. She'd never, ever been able to keep her straight-and-narrow self in check for long and now she followed her compulsion to make sure

Lenny would be inoffensive, even though she knew—she *knew,* darn it—that she was supposed to be playing it cool.

Lenny looked at her and—she could have sworn—looked empowered by the fear he'd heard in her voice. "Oh, sure," he said, with a confidence he hadn't displayed for the past fifteen minutes or so. "The Doss Man can do whatever he wants."

"Then I hope you want to succeed with Hanson," Evan said, his voice free of any signs of tension or worry. "Because that's what we have in mind."

Meredith sat and watched, ashamed of her momentary exhibition of insecurity and grateful for the fact that Evan seemed to have recovered the situation.

"So I'll be seein' ya, man," Lenny said. "And hopefully you, too," he said to Meredith, making a grand gesture of reaching for her hand and giving it a gallant medieval kiss. "Here's to our future."

She nodded and gave her most winning smile because she couldn't think of one clever or appropriate thing to say. "Welcome to Hanson," she said lamely. "I look forward to your success."

"Aw, honey, you can count on it." Lenny

tipped an imaginary cap and hauled his behind out of the bar, presumably hoping to leave his audience in awe.

Little did he know their thoughts would soon have far less to do with business than with pleasure.

Chapter Nine

Once Lenny Doss was gone, Evan and Meredith looked at each other and smiled with triumph.

"That was brilliant," Evan said, reaching for what had to be a warm beer by now. He took a gulp and set it down on the table with a bang. "Acting like at the last minute you were uncertain of the wisdom of hiring him?" He smiled, and his smile melted her heart. Or her libido. Or *something* deep inside her. "That, Ms. Waters, was genius. Pure genius."

She took just a fraction of a moment to bask in his praise before saying, "I didn't mean to do that."

Why was she confessing? Evan was impressed with her performance. She'd made a Hanson executive feel she was doing a good job. Why blow it by admitting it had almost ruined everything by a misstep? "But I'm glad it worked out."

"We make a good team," Evan said, still smiling at her. His eyes met hers and his smile faded slightly at the corners. "We always did," he added earnestly.

It would have been easy for her to come up with a smart-aleck retort but they'd fought about the past enough already. It was foolish of her to keep holding on to that when it was so long ago. She'd lived through it, grown up, finished her education, gotten a life. It wasn't the end of her life and she shouldn't act as if it was.

"That is assuming Lenny Doss is a good acquisition," she pointed out. "We may have just put a nail in Hanson Media Group's coffin."

Evan shook his head. "No way. Your instincts told you the same thing mine told me—this guy's a blowhard, but he's a blowhard with an audience. And he wants to keep his job this time." He finished his beer and put the bottle down with a hollow clatter. "Do you want anything else?" he asked, gesturing at her half-consumed wine.

"No, thanks."

It was clear he was wrapping the meeting up, and that gave Meredith a strange feeling of disappointment. She watched him gesture toward the waitress and indicate he wanted the bill.

Meredith sat back in her chair, a little unsure what to do with herself. Part of her wanted to stay with him for just a few more minutes, looking at that handsome face by the flattering light in the restaurant, but logic finally prevailed. "I'd better get going," she said, standing up and picking up her purse.

"Got a date?" Evan asked uneasily.

She smiled, without committing. "I just need to get some sleep, Evan."

"Alone?" That half smile was on his face, making her wonder if he actually cared a little or not at all.

"That's none of your business."

"I'll take that as a no."

"Take it however you want," she said, trying to sound flip but failing miserably.

"Then how about I at least walk you to your car?" he suggested.

By then they were both standing, and he put his hand on her elbow to guide her out of the restaurant.

It would have been difficult for her to deny

him that, since all he was asking was to take her to the car. It wasn't as if she could claim that an escort would slow her down so much she'd miss out on her imaginary date.

"Fine," she said. "Thanks."

"Look," Evan said, as they walked outside into the muggy summer air. Navy Pier was alive with activity, and high above them the clear night sky shone with diamondlike stars. "I know this isn't the ideal situation for you, working with me. And, truthfully, I never thought I'd be back here at all, much less asking you to help me save the company. Nevertheless, I think we did a good job together tonight. Maybe Helen was on to something when she asked you to work with me."

Meredith took a short breath inward. "Do you think she knew about our history? Did you tell her anything?"

Evan scoffed. "I hadn't talked to my father since—" he hesitated "—well, since I left, all those years ago. And probably not for a couple of weeks before that. I definitely didn't talk to Helen. Hell, she didn't show up until after I was gone."

That was true. All of Meredith's research confirmed that. Evan was merely a family member, called in at the last moment to try to salvage a company that wasn't entirely salvageable.

At least, not under its current administration.

"Do you think it was to her advantage or her disadvantage that you and I were…previously acquainted?" she couldn't resist asking. But she shouldn't have asked. She knew that from years ago: never ask a question you're not willing to hear the honest answer to.

Evan looked at her, considering. His brown eyes were warm, like melted chocolate, and Meredith figured it was the result of the beer he'd had rather than his proximity to her. "I think it was to her advantage," he said at last. "*Our* advantage, the entire company," he clarified. "You and I have a certain shorthand between us, I think. It helps in a situation like tonight's."

"Shorthand?" she repeated dumbly, though she thought she knew what he meant.

"We understand each other." He must have seen something in her that resisted that idea because he added, "Just a little bit. A little better than strangers would, anyway."

Meredith wasn't ready to agree with any of this, so instead she just let out a long sigh and said, "Maybe. I guess whatever works, we shouldn't justify it one way or the other."

Evan appeared taken aback by this, but after just a fraction of a moment, he nodded. "Yup, whatever works."

They were outside the restaurant now, close enough to hear the raucous music inside, yet far enough to feel distance from the merriment it brought most of the patrons.

Meredith turned her most confident smile on Evan. "I can get to my car myself," she said. "But thanks for thinking to walk me out, I really appre—"

She wasn't able to finish her sentence before a small, thin man—maybe a teenager—rushed past her like a cartoon villain, grabbing her purse and yanking it off her arm with such force that she actually fell to the ground.

"Meredith!" Evan was at her side in a moment. "Are you all right?"

"Yes, but—" she panted "—he took my bag. My license, credit cards…" The realization hit her like a ton of bricks. "He has my address."

"Wait here," Evan instructed, immediately on guard. "Or go back in the restaurant. I'll come back and find you."

"No, Evan, don't try to catch him," Meredith objected. "He might have friends, accomplices—"

"I don't care if he's got Tony Soprano himself waiting in the wings, he's not getting away with this."

Before she could object—and she was ready to—he had taken off, running like a thoroughbred into the night, so fast that she only saw him for a moment before he literally disappeared into the darkness.

Evan Hanson had failed her before, back when it really mattered, but now—at a time when she was at war with her memories—suddenly he was a knight in shining armor.

As soon as he was back safely and she could stop worrying that he was going to get hurt, she'd have to figure out what to think about that.

And whether she wanted to do anything about it.

It was a cheap shot.

Evan almost had him, his hand was just *inches* away from at least grabbing Meredith's purse back, if not actually clobbering the guy who took it, but apparently the mugger had an accomplice waiting for him. As he approached an alleyway he shouted something that sounded like "Yo, Carmen!" and another guy—much bigger than the first—stepped out of the shadows and sank his fist into Evan's cheekbone.

The impact stunned Evan, and he was pretty sure that for a few minutes he looked like a cartoon character, wobbling around, disoriented.

Then the guy grabbed him by the shirt—Evan heard a loud rip—and head-butted him just for good measure.

By the time he righted himself, the two assailants were long gone.

His pride might as well have been in Meredith's stolen purse as he went back to where she still stood, wringing her hands and waiting for him.

"I'm sorry," he said, holding his arms out to the side as he approached her. "They got away."

"They?"

Evan nodded as he approached. "Our pal had a friend waiting for him back by some trash dumpsters behind Melville's."

She looked at him in horror. "Oh, Evan—"

"The guy got me when I wasn't looking," he said, shaking his head. "Turns out I'm not as young or as fast as I used to be." In truth the shock on her face made him feel that much more ashamed. He *should* have been able to overtake one guy and get her bag back. "I'm sorry, Meredith."

Her eyes were still wide. "We've got to get you cleaned up, quick."

"Nah." He waved her off. "Don't worry about it. It's just a ripped shirt." He looked down, expecting to see his shirt torn open to the navel, but instead he saw his light-blue shirt had a large dark stain down the front.

Blood.

Reflexively he lifted his hand to his cheek. As soon as he did, he felt the wide gash and the slick, warm, sticky blood running from it.

That was when it *really* started to hurt.

He swore under his breath.

"You can say that again," Meredith said, moving toward him and hooking her arm through his. "My car's just in the lot over there. Do you think you can make it?"

Her touch felt nice on him, and part of him really wanted to go with her, but it wasn't necessary. "My car's just a couple of blocks away," he said. "I can get to it, don't worry."

"You are *not* driving yourself," Meredith said firmly.

"Well, I'm not bleeding all over your car."

"I've got tissues in my glove box."

Evan laughed. "That ought to take care of it."

Meredith gave him a stern look. "It will until we get you to the hospital."

"Oh, no. No way. I'm *not* going to the hospital. This is just—" he touched his cheek again and winced at the pain "—it's just a flesh wound. By tomorrow it will be invisible."

Meredith snorted and pushed him along toward her car. "Yeah, because it will probably be under more bandages than Boris Karloff had in *The Mummy*."

"That was Brendan Fraser," Evan joked.

"No, I mean the original, and anyway, Brendan Fraser wasn't the mummy in that movie, he was—" She stopped, seeing the look on his face. "Okay, you got me."

"You're so easy."

She halted in front of a small green Japanese economy car. "Yeah, well, you'll be sorry when I clean that gaping wound up with hydrogen peroxide. I may need to go over it a couple of times, just to be sure, you understand."

He groaned and got into the passenger seat where she'd pretty much pushed him. "I understand."

She shut the door and hurried over to the driver's side, her quick steps betraying her nervousness at the whole situation. Blood. Wounds. It was horrible.

"Evan, I really think we should go to the emergency room. That looks like it might need stitches."

He shook his aching head. "No, Meredith. I'm not going to wait in some overcrowded waiting room all night for treatment I could give myself."

She started the car and drove to the intersection with the main road. "Where do you live?"

It was a question he wasn't prepared to answer.

"Evan?" she prompted, when several seconds had passed and he hadn't answered yet.

How could he tell her he was sleeping in his office without sounding like a pitiful loser? Even though it made perfect sense to him because he wasn't sure he'd be sticking around long and he didn't want to commit to a yearlong lease of an apartment or condo when he might be gone in a month, saying the truth right out loud to Meredith was embarrassing at best.

But there was no way around it without sounding as if he didn't want her to know where he lived.

Which, of course, he didn't.

"If you drop me on the next corner I can just take the El."

Meredith slowed the car and turned to look at him, her left eyebrow raised. "You want me to drop you off so you, looking like that—" she made a point of looking him over "—can simply get on public transportation, frightening old ladies and small children and possibly passing out and spending the night riding aimlessly from station to station until you finally bleed to death."

He gave a half smile. "You make that sound like it's a bad idea."

She rolled her eyes. "Come on, Evan, pony up. What's the address?"

He hesitated a moment, then gave it.

She started to drive, then stopped, pulled the car over and put the transmission in park. "That's the office."

He nodded. "That's true."

"Are you trying to avoid telling me where you live, for some reason?"

He shook his head. "No, I *was* trying to avoid telling you where I live, for the simple reason that I know it sounds odd, but now you've forced it out of me."

"You live at the office."

"At the moment, yes."

"Are you serious?"

"Don't I look serious?"

"You look frightening."

He gave a concessionary nod. "That's serious."

She gripped the wheel and looked straight ahead without moving. Finally she said, "I'm going to have to take you to my house."

Evan gave a laugh. "You are taking this way, *way* too seriously. Look, just take me back to the office. I'll go clean up, slap a bandage on and be fine. Honestly, Mer, I've been in worse condition than this before. I know what I'm talking about."

Something passed between them. Whether it was surprise at his use of the old nickname, Mer, or horror at having to deal with such an indelicate situation, or simply irritation at realizing how many calls she was going to have to make to cancel credit cards, checks and so on, Evan wasn't sure.

But it sure felt…familiar.

"Evan," she said. "I think I can actually see your cheekbone through that cut."

"Oh, come on."

"God knows what I'll see in good light." She took a short breath, put the car back in gear and merged into the traffic on Lake Shore Drive. "We can clean you up at my place," she said. "If it still looks as awful as I think it's going to, I'm going to make you go to the hospital."

He knew it wouldn't, so it was an easy thing to agree to. "Fair enough."

"Okay." She drove on, and he watched her from his convenient vantage point beside her. She had to keep her eyes on the road, so he could study her profile as closely as he wanted, for as long as he wanted.

So he did.

"What are you looking at?" she asked almost immediately, glancing sideways at him.

"You," he answered softly.

"I know that. Why?"

He shifted his weight in the seat, trying to get more comfortable. "Why do you think? Because I used to know your face better than I knew my own and seeing it again after all these years is fascinating."

She shook her head. "The aging process in action."

"You're not aging, you're maturing—"

She scoffed.

"Now, wait a minute, you didn't let me finish. You've matured from a cute girl into a really beautiful woman," he said, meaning every single word of it.

In fact, he meant it more than he could say. And the realization of what he'd missed the past twelve years hit him fully, like a blow to the gut. He should have been with her through all the changes. He should have been the shoulder she cried on when her father died; he should have seen her blow out the candles on her twenty-first birthday cake; he should have been the one to put those first faint smile lines around her eyes.

There was so much he should have done for her. And with her.

So much that could never be regained.

"You're a really, seriously beautiful woman, Meredith," he found himself saying. "In every way."

Even in the dark of the car, he could tell her pale Irish skin had pinkened several shades. She tipped her head down—a gesture he'd seen her make a thousand times—so her veil of chestnut hair hid her face, at least from where he was sitting now.

"I don't know what to say, Evan."

"It's a pretty standard compliment," he said.

"'Thanks' would do. Or nothing. Nothing would do, too."

She gave a half laugh. "Thanks."

He smiled to himself. A few weeks ago, he'd had no idea he'd ever see Meredith Waters again. Then, when he first did, their interaction had filled him with dread and residual adolescent awkwardness.

But tonight something had changed.

Or maybe something had clicked into place.

Because until he'd gotten punched in the face, he'd thought he and Meredith were going to be these strange semiacquainted former lovers—until he left and she would thank the good Lord he was finally gone.

Now…it was hard to describe. But now he felt like something inside him was complete again.

Evan stayed lost in his thoughts as they drove through the familiar-yet-unfamiliar streets of his childhood. It was odd, but he still knew the timing exactly. Left on Travilia Road, left again onto Denton, bear right onto Farm Ridge, then turn left onto…

Village Crest Avenue.

Was he hallucinating?

"Meredith, where are you going?" he asked, feeling the beginnings of alarm in his chest.

"My house."

Well, yeah. Her house. Sure. He'd been there hundreds of times. He'd known the answer even before he asked the question. But the thing was, he knew it wasn't her house anymore. She'd grown up, graduated from high school, graduated from college, moved on with her life.

So clearly, either she meant something else or he was dreaming.

For a crazy second he actually wondered what year it was. The song on the radio was an old one, so that didn't help. The houses, well, they all looked the same. So that didn't help, either.

"Who's the president?" he asked stupidly.

"The president of what?"

"The United States?"

"What?"

He swallowed. It was a dumb question. He wasn't time traveling. She was just driving to her parents' house for some reason that would make sense in a few minutes.

Maybe she was driving him there because she didn't want him to know where she really lived. Or maybe she felt as if she needed help. Hell, she might have just been afraid to be alone with him. The way he probably looked, he couldn't blame her.

But now she was looking at him with something more than concern. "Okay, that's it, we need to go to the hospital *now*. I think you have a concussion."

"I don't," he said immediately, though of course he couldn't be sure.

"Then you're crazy and in need of psychiatric help. Evan, you're asking me who the *president* is!"

"I know, I was kidding. Sort of. It's just that I could swear you're driving me to…" He didn't finish his sentence. He didn't have to. She'd pulled up right in front of it.

Her parents' house.

Looking exactly as it had the last time he'd seen it, twelve and a half years ago.

Prom night.

The night he'd left Chicago and the girl of his heart, and thought it was for good.

Chapter Ten

When seeing Evan in the office, Meredith had managed to somehow separate her memories of him from the reality they were living today.

But pulling up outside the house she'd lived in when she'd dated him in high school—a house she'd only been back in for a short time now—she felt as if she were time traveling.

From the look on Evan's pale face, he was clearly feeling the same thing.

"I bought the place from my mother when she moved to Florida last year," she explained.

He looked relieved. "For a minute there, I thought I was going nuts."

She took the keys out of the ignition and said, "For a minute there, I thought you were going nuts, too."

"Thanks."

She loved his dry humor. "I should have put a Pixies CD on and asked how you did on your term paper," she continued. "As long as we didn't pass a Hummer or something, I probably could have had you going."

"You're cute," he said, getting out of the car. "Real cute."

"Uh-oh, I've been demoted." She singled out her house key as they stepped onto the front porch. "A few minutes ago you said I was beautiful."

He pointed at his head. "I was injured. I didn't know what I was saying."

"Ah." She put the key in the lock and clicked it open. "Good excuse."

They stepped into the cool, air-conditioned foyer.

Evan looked around as if he was in a time warp.

"I know," she said. "I have to redecorate. I just haven't had time. You remember where the kitchen is?"

He nodded. "Sure."

"Go on in and have a seat. I'll run and get the first-aid kit, then meet you there."

She rushed upstairs on legs that were shaking. Evan looked bad. He looked really bad. And it was all her fault, she thought, scrambling into the bathroom and throwing the cabinet doors open. Her father had always told her she had to be *way* more careful walking around downtown Chicago. He'd warned her over and over again that she was too lax about things like personal safety.

She, in turn, had told him he was paranoid, that she'd be *fine* and he just had to stop worrying so much.

She pushed around in the cabinet, moving cleaning supplies, curlers, half-used bottles of shampoo, until she finally found the white plastic box with the red cross on the front. It was about a thousand years old, but she doubted anything in it had ever been opened.

She grabbed a washcloth to clean Evan's face, thought about the amount of blood, and put the washcloth down in favor of a full-size bath towel.

Thus armed, she hurried back downstairs to the kitchen, where Evan was sitting on a stool by the counter, shirtless, still looking around in a bemused way.

He'd already cleaned the blood off his cheek and while the wound was a bit less dramatic than she'd thought, it was still more dramatic than he'd indicated. He had folded a square of paper towels that he was using to alternately apply and release pressure.

"I threw my shirt away," he said, in answer to her unasked question. "I figured it was less rude of me to sit here half-naked than to sit here in a disgusting bloody shirt."

"Good call," she said, but her mouth was suddenly dry.

His upper body was far more muscular and developed than it used to be, cut and contoured with sinewy muscle. His skin was bronzed from the sun of wherever it was he'd been this past decade, and he looked like he'd just stepped out of the pages of a *Sports Illustrated* sun-and-surf edition.

"Does it hurt?" she asked, pouring antiseptic onto a cotton pad.

"It doesn't tickle," he said, eyeing the pad dubiously.

"Neither will this," she said, gently pressing the antiseptic to the wound.

Evan cussed and drew back.

"I'm sorry!" Meredith stepped back. "It's a necessary evil. You don't want to get an infection."

He gave a rueful smile. "I'm not sure about that. It might hurt less than this."

"Yeah, until your face turns green and falls off. Come on." She put her hand on his head, her fingers touching his dark hair for the first time in ages. She swallowed, took a quick, steadying breath and said, "On the count of three."

"Don't you want to say 'this is going to hurt you a lot more than it's going to hurt me'?"

She smiled. "Sort of, but I'll refrain."

"Thank you." He winced as she put the antiseptic to his face again.

Once it was cleaned up some, a closer examination of the wound revealed that it actually wasn't quite as bad as Meredith had feared. It probably didn't need stitches. "I think one of these sealing bandages will be good enough," she said to Evan.

"I told you it wasn't so fatal."

She shrugged and took a bandage out of the first-aid kit and unwrapped it. "If it were me, I'd still go to the E.R. and make sure I don't need stitches. You might end up with a scar."

"My face isn't as pretty as yours to begin

with." He grinned. "Besides, a scar would make me look more rugged, don't you think? I'll have to make up a story that's a lot cooler than being outrun and sucker punched by a couple of punks, though. Maybe I could say I killed a guy defending a nun and a group of orphans. *Ouch!*"

"Sorry." Meredith grimaced. "It wasn't on smoothly."

"Jeez, did any skin come up with that bandage?"

"Don't worry, I've got another one." She smiled and put a new bandage on neatly. "There. Good as new. Almost."

He reached a hand up to touch the spot and grazed her hand instead. For a moment they lingered, fingertip to fingertip, and something coursed through Meredith's chest with the power of a freight train.

She drew her hand back and tried to look as if she hadn't noticed the accidental contact or felt the intense reaction.

Evan touched the spot on his cheek. "Perfect." He looked into her eyes. "You could have a future in nursing."

"I hope not," she said absently, still thinking about his touch. "I'm already working two jobs." As soon as the words left her lips, Meredith clapped her mouth shut. How could she be so stupid? She was *never* that unprofessional. It was *absolutely imperative* that she keep her secrets under wraps. And Evan Hanson was the last person in the world she should let her guard down in front of.

There was so much he must never know.

"Two jobs?" he asked, of course.

She thought fast. "Yes, working for Hanson Media and working with you." The explanation wasn't hard to come up with, but trying to make her voice sound light and casual was almost impossible.

He laughed. "I see. I'm a whole additional problem, huh?"

She let out a tense breath. He'd bought it. Thank God. "I can't believe it's the first time you've heard something like that."

"Hell, Meredith, it's not even the first time I've heard something like that from *you.*"

Thank goodness he was good-humored about it, but she really hadn't wanted to insult him. "I was only joking, Evan. You're not *that* bad."

"You're not so bad yourself." His brown eyes caught hers again and held.

Meredith's breath caught in her chest and lodged there like an iron fist. She couldn't breathe, couldn't even move, for fear of stopping something that she knew in her mind should never happen.

He was going to kiss her.

She *wanted* him to kiss her.

His gaze lingered one, two, three beats longer than she expected. Inside, she squirmed under it, hoping like a schoolgirl that he wanted her as much as she wanted him.

Finally, without saying a word, he scooped her into his arms and put his mouth over hers.

A small voice inside of her resisted, almost begging her to pull back before it was too late. Meredith knew herself well enough to know that she had never been able to resist Evan, no matter how hard she'd tried. Though years had passed and granted her more self-control where Twinkies and pizza were concerned, it seemed she still had an irresistible weakness for Evan Hanson.

She sank against him and deepened the kiss, momentarily heedless of good sense. Lots of time had passed since they'd last met like this, and part of Meredith still held the energy of waiting for him. It was as if she was righting some long-standing wrong—even though she knew in reality she couldn't do that.

Still, she could have kissed Evan for a week. A month. A year.

Twelve years.

Evan held a piece of her that had been missing all that time.

His mouth moved gently across hers, tentatively feeling for her reactions, clearly reaching the end of his ability to stop.

She didn't want him to.

His tongue touched hers, and every nerve in her body tightened like strings on a dulcimer. She ran her hands up his back, languishing in the feel of his muscled back beneath her touch, until she reached his upper back and pulled him closer to her.

Closer, something in her cried to him. *Come closer. Don't let go. This time, never let go.*

He ran strong hands down to the small of her back, holding her firmly against him. She felt safe in his embrace. It felt right. When his fingertips slipped under her shirt and pressed against her lower back, the feel of his skin touching hers in such an intimate way made her wild with desire.

As if reading her thoughts, he dipped his hand lower, sending shivers of pleasure through her core.

As Evan's mouth moved against hers and his hands played against her skin and held her close to him, Meredith felt the ache that had sat hollow in her stomach for so long finally beginning to ease.

The voice within her still tried to insist that this was wrong, that Evan had betrayed her heartlessly before and he might well do it again, but it didn't matter what she thought was wrong.

It only mattered what she felt was right.

Whoa, what was she *thinking?* Since when did Meredith Waters allow herself to do something she knew was wrong?

She pulled back abruptly. "I forgot to ask if you wanted some ibuprofen or something."

Evan looked surprised. "I'm good, thanks." He reached for her again, but she stepped back.

"Shot of whiskey?" she tried halfheartedly. "You must need something for the pain."

"No, really, Meredith, I'm fine." He eyed her, and hesitated before adding with finality, "In fact, I should call a cab or something and get out of your hair."

"No," she said quickly. Too quickly. "Evan, there's no way I'm letting you go back to sleep in the *office,* for crying out loud. You need to stay here."

He did a slight double take. "Stay here? Where here?"

"Here. Up in the guest room. In fact, you can have your pick of three guest rooms."

He raised an eyebrow. "Any of them?" he asked with a lascivious grin.

She smiled lightly. "As long as it's not already occupied."

He snapped his fingers in mock disappointment. "I hate to sleep alone."

"Yeah, and I'm guessing you haven't had to do it that often, either." She was joking, but something about the words stuck in her craw a little bit.

"More than you'd think, Meredith," he answered, his voice serious.

Their eyes met, and a frisson of energy zapped between them.

She could have thrown herself right back into his arms and kissed him until she forgot about every other thing in her life and in the outside world, but she knew better.

She had to keep *reminding* herself, of course, but she definitely knew better.

"Anyway," she said pointedly. "The fact is that tonight you'll be sleeping alone and you'll be doing it here."

"That's really not necessary."

"What kind of person would let someone risk life and limb to get a stupid purse back and then just send him on his way?" She shook her head. "Not me. Now get upstairs, mister. You need to rest."

He stood up and faltered, losing his balance ever so slightly, but enough for her to say, "See? That proves my point."

"Yes, ma'am."

"I have some big old T-shirts," she went on. "I'll get you one and you can sleep in that."

"I sleep naked," he said, a sly grin playing on his lips. "Have you forgotten?"

She sucked in a breath. No, she hadn't forgotten. When she was sleeping with him, *she* slept nude as well.

It saved time.

But she wasn't going to think about that and she wasn't going to give Evan any indication that she'd thought about it, so she simply said, "I thought the circumstances might make you more modest."

"The circumstances are making me more…" He shook his head. "Well, anyway, I get the point."

"Good. Keep it covered. There's a bathrobe on the door of the bathroom. You can put that on and toss me your jeans and…everything. I'll wash them."

"You really don't have to do that."

"Stop saying that. Just give me the clothes, would you?"

"You've sure gotten bossy over the years."

"Evan."

He put his hands up in surrender. "Okay, okay, I hear you. I'll strip for you. No problem."

She sighed. "You know all that stuff I said about being able to work with you?"

"Uh-huh."

"I'm starting to think I should ask for a raise." She smiled. "They're not paying me enough for this."

He laughed. "I'll talk to the boss on your behalf."

"Good." She led him to the bottom of the staircase. "Now go. Toss your stuff down to me when you've got it off."

"Fine." He made his way up the stairs and she leaned against the wall and waited for him.

About two minutes later he tossed his things down and said, "No starch!"

It was going to be a long night.

Chapter Eleven

It was a strange feeling having Evan Hanson sleeping in her house.

A very strange feeling.

As Meredith sat by the washer and dryer, waiting for them to complete their cycles so she could take Evan's clothes to his room and go to sleep, she had to keep reminding herself that this was all really happening.

There was once a time when she would never have imagined herself forgiving him and facing him again, but that was fading now. It wasn't Evan's fault that her father's business had been ruined, it was George Hanson's. The more she dug around Hanson Media Group, and the more people she spoke with, the more obvious it was that he had been a completely ruthless business-man for whom nothing was personal and every-thing had been war.

Now, instead of blaming Evan for his father's misdeeds, she pitied him for having had that sort of man for a father. As rough as it was to compete with him in business, it had to be almost as rough to live up to his standards as a son.

As a matter of fact, she remembered some of Evan's struggle with George Hanson. Not that Evan had talked about it much, but he'd gone through periods of quiet introspection that had worried her sometimes, and it wasn't until she'd drawn him out that she knew it was because of his father's heavy hand.

For her, it was just one more thing to hate about George Hanson.

When she'd taken this job, she'd thought it would be easy because of the unpleasant con-notations she had with the Hanson family name. She thought she'd feel no hint of conscience or betrayal because any personal warm feelings she'd had for anyone in the family had long since died and been replaced by the opposite.

In a way it had seemed like the perfect opportunity to get back at them, even though they'd never know it was her.

Now...well. Now things were getting a little more complicated. She'd still do her job; she was nothing if not professional.

But she was going to have to get some perspective where Evan was concerned. And that she would get by reminding herself how, even though he didn't have anything to do with the greatest tragedy of her life—her father's ruin and death—he was *directly* responsible for the greatest heartbreak of her life.

There was no way around that one.

The dryer stopped and she took the warm jeans out. Size 32 waist. He'd filled out.

But of course she knew that.

She started up the stairs and remembered a conversation she'd had with him once. The memory hit her with crystal clarity and hit her so hard she had to stop and sit down.

They'd snuck out in the night once because it had seemed so romantic. It had been her idea, as she recalled, but Evan had indulged her. He'd come to her window at 2:00 a.m. and she'd climbed down the trellis, just like a cliché in a movie.

It was summer, and hot. Even the nights were hot, and the air was damp with humidity. They'd gone to a small private cove he knew of on Lake Michigan and they'd sat on the beach and talked for hours.

She couldn't remember most of what they'd said. It was a lot of talk about their pasts, their dreams and the other typical things that kids that age could expound upon.

She remembered the night specifically because a quick but wild thunderstorm had come out of the blue, interrupting the clear starry night with about ten minutes of drama.

Kissing in that thunderstorm had been one of the most romantic moments of her life.

It was amazing that she could remember anything else, but she did. Evan had asked her if her father had ever thought about selling his newspaper business.

"I don't know. Why?"

Evan had shrugged. But now, when she saw it again in her memory, she realized he had looked tense.

"Just seems like a really competitive business. I've heard sometimes it gets ugly, one paper accusing another of publishing lies and whatnot. It's hard for a newspaper to come back after that kind of accusation."

She'd laughed—laughed!—seeing no significance in what he was saying at all.

"Oh, come on, Evan, no one takes that stuff that seriously. Look at all the tabloids at the grocery store that say aliens are walking among us. Everyone knows they're full of lies, but they're still in business."

"It's different, Meredith. I wouldn't want to be in the news business for anything. I'd hate to see a nice guy like your dad get into trouble in business."

"As long as he keeps the aliens off the front page, he'll be fine." She could remember saying that, because then she'd looked up and seen a shooting star.

She'd wished for a long, happy future with Evan.

Maybe the star had been an alien.

She started up the stairs with his warm clothes now, playing and replaying his words in her head. How on earth had she forgotten that hugely significant conversation until now?

Or, on the other hand, how had she remembered it at all? Given how little thought she'd put into it at the time, and how many other things had happened that night that were a lot more interesting to the mind of a teenage girl, she was amazed that it was still in her head at all.

She wondered if Evan remembered.

She stopped at the door to the guest room she'd directed him to and knocked softly.

No answer.

Slowly she opened the door and peeked in. Light from the bathroom spilled in and she could see he was on his side, breathing softly and rhythmically.

She set his clothes down on the dresser and started to leave but then she turned back.

As if watching someone else, and completely incapable of stopping them, she walked back over to the side of the bed and looked down at him. She told herself she just wanted to make sure he seemed all right, in case he had a concussion, but the truth was she wanted to be closer to him, to see him without his knowing it.

It might have been ten minutes that she stood there, looking at that handsome face half hidden by the shadows of the night. It was a face she'd thought about many times over the years. At first with love, then later with pain and confusion, then finally with anger.

Now she wasn't sure how she felt.

And that scared her more than anything.

She turned to leave and stepped on a creaky floorboard that protested loudly.

She froze, listening for the even breath of his sleep.

Instead she heard his voice. "Meredith?"

She turned back to him. "I just brought your clothes back. They're on the dresser."

He looked through sleepy eyes at the dresser across the room, then back at her by the bed and clearly not anywhere near the clothes.

"Then I came to check on you and make sure you were breathing normally," she explained in answer to his unasked question. "You know, all the typical concussion checks. Steady breathing, ability to wake up. Congratulations, you passed."

He sat up in bed and the sheets fell away from him, revealing a bare torso.

So much for the T-shirts she'd offered him.

And so much for her resolve to keep a professional distance from him. This was a sight that would easily fuel the romantic fantasies of any red-blooded American woman, and it was right here in her own house.

"Thanks," he said. "Am I okay?"

"I think you'll live."

"Can't ask for more than that, I guess."

This was hard, all this small talk in a room filled with such big tension.

"If there's nothing you need, I'll be going to sleep now," she said to him. She swallowed. "Do you need anything?"

Three heartbeats passed.

"There is one thing…."

"What is it?"

"I—" He stopped. "Never mind. It's nothing."

"Oh. Okay. If you're sure…"

He nodded.

"Good night, then."

"Good night."

She started to go, then stopped and turned back. She had to ask him this. If she didn't, it would drive her crazy. "Evan?"

"Hmm?" He sat up again.

"Can we talk for a minute?"

"Sure." He scooted back in the bed. "Have a seat."

She went over and sat on the edge of the bed, facing him. "I want you to be absolutely honest, okay?"

He frowned. "Okay."

"Did you know what your father was planning to do to my father's business?"

He blew air into his cheeks, then let it out in a long, tense stream. "I guess we were going to get to this someday."

"So you did."

"I had an idea, yeah."

"An idea? Or you *knew?*" The possibilities mounted in her mind. "Did he tell you?"

He raked his hand through his hair and looked at her. "You sure you want to do this?"

Her stomach began to feel shaky and upset. It was like getting a phone call and knowing it was bad news before even picking up the receiver. "Tell me," she said.

"I knew my father wanted to buy your father's paper. Everyone knew that. He even made an offer, but your dad refused."

"He loved his work."

"I know," Evan said softly. "It wasn't his fault."

"Obviously not," she said, a tad too defensively. "So your father told you he was going to plant lies about my father's paper to cast doubt on the credibility?"

"No, he didn't tell me." He was choosing his words carefully, talking slowly.

Meredith wanted answers now. "Then how did you know?"

"I heard him talking to someone on the

phone one night. It wasn't hard to put two and two together and figure out what he was planning to do." He shook his head. "I tried to warn you one night—"

"At the beach?"

"That's right." He nodded. "You remember that?"

"It only just occurred to me." She shifted her weight, and the mattress squeaked. "But if you knew, why didn't you tell me directly? You were so vague…. I had *no idea* you were trying to make me aware of something so important." Her eyes burned but she wouldn't cry. "Why didn't you just *tell* me?"

There was a long moment where Evan said nothing. Then at last he said, "Because I was a kid, Meredith. I didn't have firsthand information about the plan, and even if I did, we're talking about betraying my father." He shook his head again, the slow movement showing his regret. "I thought I needed to be loyal to my family. To my father."

A terrible thought occurred to her. "Did our relationship…did it have anything to do with helping your father take over my father's company?"

"Of course not," Evan said, clearly offended at the suggestion.

Relief coursed through Meredith, calming her tight stomach.

But it was short-lived.

"I would never have dated you in order to help my father get access to the newspaper," Evan went on. "In fact, when he suggested our relationship could be of use to him, I ended it."

She felt like she'd been punched in the stomach. Had she heard that correctly? "Wait a minute. You're saying you left because your father wanted to use us to gain access to my father's business?"

Evan nodded slowly. "That's exactly what I'm saying."

Chapter Twelve

It was the first time in her life Meredith had ever even *thought* about quitting a job halfway through. Her job description of corporate researcher had a lot of mutations, and while she wasn't usually a corporate spy—or, as some put it, *competitive intelligence agent*—it wasn't unheard of for her.

As long as she felt comfortable with the reasons for her research and believed she wasn't breaching her own personal morals and standards she was able to do a good job.

This time, though, things were getting foggy. She'd told her employer she might have a conflict of interest, and her employer had guessed right off that it might have something to do with her relationship with Evan.

It was hard for Meredith to explain that it did because of something that had happened a long, long time ago. How could she say that she'd just learned he'd once had the chance to do almost the same thing to her that she was doing to him and he'd opted not to?

It sounded so…unprofessional.

So she'd had to settle for explaining that she'd never before taken this kind of job with a company she had any personal relationship with—even a relationship as tangential and outdated as the one she had with the Hansons—and that she was finding it more difficult than she'd anticipated to completely fulfill her obligations to everyone involved.

Especially when the end result would be the hostile takeover of Evan's company.

To Meredith's surprise her employer had assured her that there was *no* hostile takeover in the works. That they were seeking a merger—a way to take two strong companies and put them together to make them both even more powerful.

Hanson Media Group wasn't going to lose

in this deal, Meredith was told—they were going to win.

That was believable, Meredith supposed. Hanson could accept an offer to share partnership instead of being subject to a hostile takeover and thereby having no choice.

"So are you prepared to stay on and finish the job you began?" her employer had asked.

The sixty-four-thousand—only in this case it was more like million—dollar question.

Meredith thought about it for a moment. Her instincts told her she could believe what she was being told, and in the past few years her instincts had become pretty good.

"Yes," she said at last. "I am. You can depend on me."

Evan was starting to have a hard time getting his thoughts straight.

Being at Meredith's parents' house the other night was just too strange. How many hours had he spent there in his lifetime, enjoying the company of the girl he had once been absolutely sure he'd marry?

It was weird to come back, now that she was a grown woman—a woman who had spent more than a decade growing away from him—and see her in that same environment.

It gave him a strange feeling, a combination of unease and melancholy.

Not to mention the all-new desire he felt for Meredith as she fit right into his life and his mind now. The way she'd handled Lenny Doss was amazing. More to the point, the way she handled everything at work was amazing. She was a perfect professional, always conservative but always right.

It was ironic that the very quality that had driven him crazy when they were dating—her unwillingness to take a risk—was the very thing he appreciated in her now.

After he'd spent the night in her guest room, he'd gotten up early, written a note of thanks and called a cab to take him back to his car at Navy Pier. It was better that way, he figured: no awkward morning talk, no uncomfortable silences.

He'd been at work for three and a half hours, with no sign of Meredith, when he finally decided to take a casual look around for her.

But she wasn't in the PR offices, and David said he hadn't seen her all day. So when Evan

found her at a lone computer at the far end of
the accounting department, he was puzzled.

He watched her for a few minutes from a
distance, clicking on the computer keyboard,
squinting and looking closer, then jotting notes
down on a pad in front of her.

Now what was *that* all about?

He moved closer, hoping to catch a better
glimpse of her work without making his presence so obvious that, if caught, he couldn't say
he'd just wandered in.

So very carefully he walked up behind her
and tried to see what was on the computer
screen.

Revenues. Debt. Balances.

Meredith was studying the entire financial
profile of the company.

Why?

He backed off again, unnoticed, to contem-
plate his next move in the hallway.

Was Meredith a corporate spy of some sort?

No, that was too absurd. What had made him
even think such a thing? Meredith was far too
principled to be dishonest in any capacity, much
less lie to someone's face, as she would have to
with Evan, David, Helen and everyone else she
came into contact with at the office.

Come on.

It was far more likely that ever-responsible-and-forward-thinking Meredith was checking out the company's vital statistics because she was interested in some personal investing, rather than reporting back to some supersecret source.

If anyone was bold enough to take a chance on investing in a company at rock bottom, it was Meredith. She'd see, as he did, that Hanson Media would rebound one way or another.

That was definitely more in keeping with Meredith's personality, yet…Evan wasn't quite sure. Something about this didn't sit right with him. An investor would have plenty of ways to monitor the debt-to-income ratio and the viability of the company as a potential investment. There were books, Web sites, portfolios and, hell, *people* who dedicated their entire existence to providing that kind of information.

Still, the idea of Meredith checking the company information for some sort of nefarious intention was unlikely in the extreme.

He'd have to keep an eye on the situation. He'd keep Meredith close and see if he could figure out what she was up to without his ever having to ask.

* * *

Several days passed since Evan had stayed at Meredith's house, and they never really talked about it again. His cut healed fairly quickly, she was glad to see. He'd probably been right: she was too paranoid in suggesting he needed to go to the hospital right away for stitches.

The strange thing was, he was barely talking to her.

Despite the great strides he'd made in the company—after getting Lenny Doss, he'd managed to secure contracts with three other famous names, including the Alleyway Guys, who had a popular, irreverent car talk show—his conversations with Meredith were brief and to the point.

She couldn't argue with his professional decisions, so it wasn't as if he had that to worry about. The Alleyway Guys, at least, wouldn't be as great a liability as Lenny Doss could be, and the radio psychologist he'd hired had a reputation for being aggressively conservative, but that always ended up making for good listening, both because of the callers who disagreed with her *and* the callers who agreed.

So the radio division was shaping up. Despite the risks involved—and they were many—the acquisition of Lenny Doss would probably be a profitable one. Evan was smart to create an interesting but reliable mix of talent. All of them were proven talents with good, solid numbers behind them.

That would undoubtedly help with her employers' plans for a merger.

"So how's everything going over at the Web site?" she asked David, late in the afternoon. It was almost time to go, and she hoped it would sound like a casual question that he could answer and then leave without thinking too much.

"Actually, things are great," David said. "All squared away. Hanson Media Group is on its way back."

"Really? What do you attribute that to?"

David hesitated. "I guess it's everything combined. The family has come in and worked really hard to save the company, and I think it's showing in every department. We're not in the clear yet, of course, but things are really looking up."

Meredith smiled. "So you think the company can survive on its own?"

David looked at her sharply. "As opposed to what?"

She'd spoken too fast. "I mean you won't need to file for chapter eleven or get a loan?"

David narrowed his eyes and looked at her. "Are you worried about keeping your job?"

She was relieved that that was his only question. She opened her arms into a wide shrug and said, "I'm a single woman working to pay for a house and make my way in this world." She smiled. "It ain't easy. Any reassurance you could give me about job security would be greatly appreciated." She hated to lie to him that way—job security was the least of her worries—but she needed his input on how the company was doing. David Hanson's word was gold within the industry, and she needed a little of that rich, shiny news to take back to her employer.

"I can't assure you of anything," David said, to her disappointment. "This is a wildly uncertain business struggling in wildly uncertain times. However, I can tell you that the public interest in Evan's programming is high. The kid has good instincts, just like Helen figured he would."

"He's a little reckless," Meredith interjected, with a ping of conscience at saying something potentially negative about Evan.

"*Ambitious* might be a better way of putting that," David said gently. "He's been working against the odds, and against the opposition of many within the company, but he's still arranged for a lineup he feels good about, and the industry buzz is on his side." David shrugged broadly. "How do we argue with that?"

"Hopefully, we don't," Meredith agreed. It was a good recommendation of Evan and his work, and she knew David Hanson was far too meticulous a professional to say anything he didn't mean, just to flatter his nephew.

"So the company's in good shape?" She was careful to sound interested but not too eager. "It's not about to go down the tubes or anything?"

"It's all good," David said shortly, but with what sounded like confidence. "No worries."

"Well, good," Meredith said with a smile. "I'm glad to know I'll be safely employed in the immediate future."

"You can count on it," David said, looking her in the eye.

And she already knew it. She *was* safely employed. The question was, how many people at Hanson Media Group could say the same thing?

Not too many.

* * *

She was asking a lot of questions, Evan noticed. Questions that *could* be normal, in the line of business, but which seemed just a little bit…outside the bounds of her job.

It wasn't as if he could take a lot of time to follow her around, though, to see what she was up to. Evan still had his own job to do, and after a decade of killing time all day until his bartending shift at night, he wasn't too keen on the idea of figuring out why anyone should want to the know the Arbitron ratings for the last three years when it was his primary concern to make sure the *next* three years were more successful.

And somehow he had to do that with Meredith Waters by his side, driving him to distraction with almost every breath she took.

He'd never forgotten her, of course. He didn't even try to fool himself about that one. But what was really striking him was how interested in her he was getting *again*. It wasn't just the shadow she cast in his past—she had grown into a fascinating and exciting woman. A strange blend of professional savvy and goofy good humor.

There were more facets to her than he could count. And he wanted to learn about them all.

Was it just because of what they'd shared

once? Was all of the heat he felt between them simply a matter of a once-sizzling love affair? Or was it possible that what he'd seen in her once was something that he needed still, something that complemented his soul in a way that was to be profound all his life?

He turned the thought over in his mind and tried to imagine how they could possibly be together now, even theoretically. He wasn't going to be here long. Chicago held nothing for him. God alone knew where he'd go next, but it was a fairly safe bet that Meredith wouldn't want to join him. She had her life here. Her career was here. And one thing about Meredith that didn't seem to have changed was her inclination to be a homebody.

So there was probably nothing more to say about it than that. The past was the past, and Evan was going to have to get a grip on himself and stop fantasizing about the girl who got away. He'd let her go and there was no getting her back now.

Both he and Meredith needed to look toward the future. Of Hanson Media Group, that is.

Nothing more.

Why couldn't she get her mind off him?

Meredith sat in her office, trying to do the advertising analysis that David had asked her to do. But all she could concentrate on was Evan.

And he wasn't even around.

Well, he was *around,* somewhere in the office, but she'd barely seen him, except for running into him occasionally when she was alone in the copy room and again when she was returning from an early lunch. Both times Evan had been cordial, polite, but basically he'd acted as if they were strangers.

Was he *mad* at her?

The last time they'd really spoken he'd admitted that he'd known his father's intention had been to sabotage her father's business. Or at least he'd *suspected* it, and that was enough for Meredith. He'd had an inkling of what was to come, but he'd barely alluded to it in conversation, much less actually come out and *warned* her.

She *should* be mad at him.

But she wasn't. That was ancient history now, and whatever his culpability for not revealing what he suspected, he had been part of George Hanson's campaign to steal her father's newspaper and, in fact, after warning her in his far-too-subtle way, he'd left the country. So even the greatest cynic couldn't say he was actually *part of* the conspiracy.

So, no, she wasn't mad. Not at Evan. Not for that. Not anymore.

Instead she found herself watching for him every time she heard footsteps in the hall. When someone entered the room, she looked up quickly, hoping it was him. And when it wasn't, as it inevitably wasn't, she was disappointed.

What was going on here?

Finally, at almost five o'clock in the afternoon, when she was about to seek him out and ask if and why he was avoiding her, Evan knocked on her door and poked his head in. "Got a minute?"

She should have been cool and professional but she was so glad to see him that she couldn't help the excited smile she felt on her face. "Sure."

He came in. "I was hoping you might go out with me and grab a bite to eat. There's something—" he hesitated "—there's something I want to talk to you about."

She frowned. "Sounds serious."

"It's not that big a deal. I just thought it would be nice to get out of the office. I'm not used to being trapped under fluorescent lighting all the time."

"I guess it doesn't compare to the Mediterranean sun." There was a tiny sharp edge to her voice, and she hoped he wouldn't notice it.

However, the quick glance he gave her said he had. "You should try it sometime."

"Maybe I will."

He raised an eyebrow. "Really?"

"Why do you sound so surprised?"

"I'm not, I just… You never expressed much interest in travel before."

She shrugged. "I've never in my life had the time to travel. First it was school, then it was work, now it's like some pathological habit. I think it's time I broke it."

He smiled, the smile that had always made her heart flip. "Starting tonight, then. We'll go to a little Greek restaurant I know on the outskirts of town."

She was ready to go farther than that. At this moment, she could have gotten on a plane and taken off for Greece itself, with nothing more than a bathing suit and some sunscreen.

Of course, the image was so unlike her it was almost funny, but suddenly she found herself—unexpectedly and uncharacteristically—hungry for something new, and Chicago just wasn't offering it to her.

Maybe tonight it would at least give her a little taste.

"Should I change my clothes?" she asked, feeling unexpectedly girlish at his offer.

Evan looked her over, and her skin prickled in response, as if he'd touched her. "No, you're fine."

Fine. It wasn't high praise, but it would do. Especially given the way he'd looked at her.

"Okay, then." She shut her computer down and picked up her purse. "I'm ready if you are."

They took the elevator down to the parking garage and went to Evan's car. He went to open the door for her and she mused, "It's been a long time since someone opened a door for me."

"Chivalry's dead, huh?"

"That or it's been asleep." She got into the car and leaned back against the buttery soft leather seats. "Sound asleep."

"So." Evan started the car. "Do you date a lot?"

She was taken by surprise at his question. "Do I *date* a lot?"

He nodded, his eyes on the road in front of him. "Or is that an inappropriate question."

"I don't know if it is or not." She thought for a minute. "Do *you* date a lot?"

He gave a laugh and glanced at her sideways. "Never mind, that *is* a hard question to answer."

"Because there have been so many?" She was unable to stop herself from asking.

"Hardly."

But she wasn't sure she believed him.

"Let me try this one," he said after a couple of moments had passed. "Have you been married? Engaged?"

This was so weird to be talking to Evan about this. "I was engaged once," she said, though part of her didn't want to confess it to him for some reason. "But it didn't work out."

"Why not?"

She looked out the window and gave a dry laugh. "He wasn't ambitious. Didn't have solid plans for the future. I was afraid he might not be…reliable."

The single moment that passed before Evan spoke was so rife with tension that she had no doubt he understood the irony of her failed relationship.

"Maybe you just expected too much of him."

"Certain expectations are so basic that to call them 'too much' is ludicrous." She kept her gaze fastened on the road, watching the yellow lines on the black street disappear under the car. But inside she was thinking, *Please give me a good explanation for what you did, please make me understand.*

"Sometimes people can't fulfill basic expectations for really good reasons," Evan said. "Sometimes things are different from what you think."

"All I know is what I see," she countered, wishing it was enough to believe him but knowing she needed something more. Something concrete. "It's hard to speculate about 'theoretically' when the facts are slapping you in the face."

He took a deep breath. "If they're really the facts. In our case, I just…" He lost the words and shook his head. "It doesn't matter. We're not talking about us."

Meredith stiffened in her seat. She felt her face flush hotly. She was far too ready to talk about them. It just wasn't healthy. He'd moved on. And she'd thought she had, as well.

She just needed to remind herself of that now and then. "Of course not. That was a long time ago. It has nothing to do with now."

"Right."

She couldn't help goosing him a little. "Despite how defensive you seem to be about the past sometimes."

A mile passed.

"Look," Evan said. "I'm sorry. We were talking about your fiancé, and I turned it into my own postmortem defense. It really wasn't appropriate and I apologize for that. I was…just remembering."

"I remember sometimes, too, Evan." *Please make me understand, please make it believable.*

He swung the car in past the Sophie's sign at the entry to a dingy parking lot and slowed to a halt. Then he turned in his seat and said, "Do you?"

She gave a half smile. "I'm not senile."

"Do you ever have any regrets?"

"No," she answered firmly.

They eyes locked, then slowly Evan moved toward her. Meredith sat still, not drawing back, even though her mind screamed for her to run.

Okay, don't make me believe. Just kiss me and make me forget.

His lips grazed lightly across hers, suggesting the satiation of a desire that had gone unanswered for much too long.

A moment rested in stillness, then Evan's mouth descended on hers again, but this time it was more fervent. He moved his mouth across hers in a hungry, almost urgent, way, drawing her in by the sheer force of his passion.

His tongue touched hers, and the taste of him sent a shock of remembrance through her core.

She trailed her hands across his upper back and curled them around his neck, resting her arms on his broad shoulders. He pulled her closer, moving his hands across her body and hungrily exploring her mouth with his own.

The sound of their mingled breaths increased as their ardor grew.

Evan ran a strong hand down to the small of Meredith's back, and she arched toward him, hitting the hard console between them. She didn't care. The pleasure outweighed the pain by a hundredfold. His fingertips dipped lightly inside her panties, and an explosion of excitement arched Meredith's back and she gasped against his mouth.

"I want you," he whispered to her.

"I want you, too," she said, ignoring the tiny voice of conscience that insisted this was a mistake.

Evan's kisses deepened and a pulse throbbed in the pit of Meredith's stomach, extending to her core. It was an ache that only he could reach and she was half ready to let him do it right here and right now.

Evan slipped his hands under Meredith's shirt and swept them across the bare skin of her back and down again. Her breath caught in her throat. She wanted him.

Oh, how she wanted him.

And she'd *told* him so.

She realized with sudden horror what she was doing and how crazy it was. She drew back, nearly slamming her head into the window behind her.

"We can't do this," she gasped.

"Yes, we can." He reached for her again and kissed her.

She gave in to it for one languorous moment, then pushed back again. "No, we can't. I don't want to."

"I don't believe you."

She took a short breath that betrayed her truth. "You have to."

"I have to respect the word *no*," he said. "I don't have to believe you mean it. Even if I didn't know you before, Meredith, what we just had spoke volumes. Your body told me everything you're not willing to admit."

"*That*—" she gestured lamely "—what just

happened was…it was meaningless. Curiosity, nothing more." She swallowed, then continued. "Now that we've gotten it out of our systems, it must never happen again."

"It sure as hell isn't out of my system," Evan said. "In fact, ever since I saw you again, you've been slowly working your way right back into my system. It's almost like—"

"Don't say it." She raised a hand. She didn't want to hear it was like old times or that it was as if nothing had changed or, worse, it was like they were meeting for the first time. "Don't say it. There's no way you can finish that sentence without sounding like a line from every melodramatic movie ever made."

Evan gave a sharp laugh. "Thanks."

Warmth washed over her face. "You know what I mean. Don't you?"

"Maybe. What I don't know is why you're so damn eager to ignore what your heart is telling you."

"Who said my heart was involved in this transaction?"

"Okay, your body." He gave a rakish grin. "I'll take that."

No you won't. I'm not giving it again. "No

way. There's nothing to gain by getting involved in something that we both know can never work."

"You don't know that."

"I do. Look, Evan, you left once without saying a word. I wasn't enough for you then, and there's no reason to think things would be different now. "

He straightened his back and looked out the window in front of him. "I didn't leave because you weren't enough for me. It was nothing like that."

"Then what was it?"

He looked at her, his face shadowed by the twilight. "It was complicated."

"Too complicated to explain?"

"What's the point?"

"I don't know." She couldn't admit that she wanted the peace of mind of knowing. It sounded too pathetic. "Maybe there isn't one."

There passed a moment of eye contact between the two of them that sent shivers rushing up and down Meredith's spine. He looked as if he was going to kiss her again.

More to the point, she wanted him to kiss her again; she wanted to feel herself in his arms again; she wanted to feel that rough beard against her cheek. Heat pulsed between the two of them.

He moved toward her and she leaned in ever so slightly until he was just the merest breath away.

Then her phone rang.

She started in surprise. Who would be calling her at this hour?

Her first thought was that it might be an emergency, something to do with her mother.

"I'm sorry," she said to Evan, fumbling through her purse. "I have to get this. It could be my mom."

She answered the phone.

"I'm sorry to call so late," the voice on the other end of the line said. "But I'm getting ready to leave for Japan and I need to know if you finished assembling the data you were working on about Hanson Media Group."

Chapter Thirteen

Meredith moved the phone to her other ear and subtly turned the volume on the earpiece down. "I don't have that information with me right now. I can go home and get it, though, if you need me to."

"You're not alone?"

"Um…no."

"I need to talk to you about this. Can you call me back soon, in private?"

She didn't want to, but Meredith knew she really had no choice. "All of those records are at home, Mother." She hated having to stoop so low as to pretend it was her mother. "Can it wait until morning?"

"Sorry, you have to do this now."

"Okay, let me just call you back in—" she glanced at her watch "—about forty-five minutes. Is that okay?"

"That's fine. But sooner is better. Try and hurry, Meredith, okay?"

"You got it." She gave Evan an exasperated look as she flipped the phone shut and put it back into her purse. "I'm sorry, I've got to get back home and get some documentation together for my mother. Something to do with her new housing situation and needing to prove she sold her assets out here."

Evan nodded. "I'll take you home right away."

That just seemed wrong. With everything she was doing she couldn't bear to make him feel like he had to accommodate her. "No, no, I know you were looking forward to eating here. It's not a big deal for me to take a cab back to the office and drive home. Heck, I'd walk if I had the time."

"Meredith, I'm not letting you take a cab back to the office so I can go get myself some souvlaki. I'll drive you."

"You don't—"

"Don't be ridiculous," he interrupted. He started the car and put it in gear. "This isn't a big deal."

"Well, thanks."

He pulled out of the parking lot. "Is everything okay with your mom?"

"What? Oh. Yes. Fine. It's just—" She had to tell herself this really was about her mother, that it was routine personal business and not something that could affect Evan or his family. "She's constantly needing one document or another from the house. She left a ton of stuff behind." That much, at least, was true.

"Your mom is lucky to have you," Evan said as he drove. "After she lost your dad, she must have been really lost."

"She was," Meredith agreed.

"I remember how close they were," Evan continued, smiling more to himself than Meredith. "They'd be worse than teenagers at the dinner table, laughing and finishing each other's sentences."

Meredith smiled, remembering. "I always thought that was the definition—"

"—of true love, yeah," Evan agreed, apparently unaware that he had just finished Meredith's sentence himself.

But she was aware of it.

"When you know each other so well, *and* agree with each other so completely, that you can finish each other's sentences," he went on, "that really shows a certain comfort level. It's enviable, really."

"Yes," she agreed, looking at him through the darkness, illuminated only occasionally by the streetlights they passed. "I think you're right."

"It probably had a lot to do with how you turned out."

"Meaning…?"

"You have always been secure in yourself, Meredith. Some might even say a little bull-headed—" he gave a quick smile "—but definitely secure with who you are and what you think. I think that comes from growing up in a house where everyone was loved and accepted for who they were."

"As opposed to how you grew up?" she asked, before she could think better of it.

He didn't even hesitate to answer. "Definitely. I knew before I could talk that I had to watch what I said around my father. The strain of keeping us all quiet and agreeable for him probably had a lot to do with my mother's eventual illness."

And death, Meredith thought, but she didn't say it. She didn't have to. She knew they were both thinking it. "You must have had some good times with your family," she ventured. "It's not like you were a miserable kid."

"Not when I was with you." He kept his eyes on the road and his hands on the wheel. "Maybe whatever you had in your upbringing spilled over to me when we were together. The only time I really felt comfortable back then was when I was with you."

The thought warmed her heart, even while it rang every warning bell within her. "It obviously didn't mean *that* much to you," she said. "You didn't have too hard a time leaving it."

He drew to a halt at a stoplight and looked at her, the red hue illuminating his left cheek, casting shadows that made him look older. *"That,"* he said, "is not true."

Once again she found herself wishing he'd explain. Yet even while she wished, she didn't want him to. "No? Then how did you do it? Evan, you never looked back. No call, no letter, no message in a bottle."

"It was best for you that you didn't hear from me."

She scoffed. "*Best* for me? Who do you think you're kidding?"

"It was," he insisted. The car behind them honked its horn and Evan looked up to see the light had changed. He drove forward and went on, saying to Meredith, "You'll just have to trust me on this."

"Evan, we're grown people now. This happened more than a decade ago. I'd like to know what happened. This cryptic 'it was best for you' business just doesn't cut it. Either tell me the truth or don't talk about the past at all."

"You're right. We shouldn't talk about it at all."

She sighed. "Just *tell me the truth.*"

He laughed lightly. "Fine, Meredith. It's simple. My father wanted to use our relationship, yours and mine, to his advantage over your father. He wanted me to get information on your father's writers, the stories they were coming up with, how best to get in there and switch the facts around and cast doubt on your father's credibility."

Meredith felt the blood leave her face. "He wanted you to *spy* for him?"

"Essentially, yes. Though that's a pretty dramatic label." He blew a long breath out. "Either way, what it would have come down to was me using you, or appearing to." The next light turned yellow, and Evan slowed the car again.

"Why didn't you tell me?"

He looked at her. "Because I was eighteen and I didn't know how to betray my father like that."

"But you could betray me."

"I *didn't* betray you. I left the country. I cut out of the whole deal so I wasn't part of hurting *anyone*."

Which felt to her like a betrayal of the highest order. He *had* hurt her, and he still didn't seem to realize it. "It was pretty damn easy for you," she said, hating the bitter edge to her voice, even though she couldn't soften it.

He shook his head. "It was the hardest thing I ever had to do!"

"But…?"

His gaze landed evenly on her. "But I did it. It was the best I could do for everyone."

This wasn't going anyplace good. Meredith *knew* she shouldn't have indulged her impulse to talk to him about this. It made her regress to an angry, confused teenager, and she had gotten so far away from that until Evan had reappeared.

She didn't want to be this person.

"Okay, okay. *Uncle,*" she said, glad to see they were approaching the entrance to the office building's garage. "We're not getting anywhere with this conversation."

"Agreed."

"So let's drop it."

He gave a single nod. "Consider it dropped."

The entered the grungy grey garage in silence, the dim fluorescent lighting acting as the perfect punctuation to Meredith's dissatisfaction.

"Okay." She pointed to her little blue sports car. "That's it right there."

"I remember." He pulled the car up behind hers and turned to her. "Here you go."

"Thanks." She started to get out of the car, then stopped and turned back to him. "I'm sorry I had to cut dinner off. I hope you're not starving."

"I'll survive." He smiled. "I'll just drive through and get a burger somewhere."

She nodded. "Good night, Evan."

He looked at her evenly, his gaze inscrutable. "Good night."

She got out of the car and felt him watching her as she unlocked the doors, got in and started the ignition. He pulled his car away, and she backed up and followed him out of the garage. He turned right and drove off in the opposite direction of where she was going.

She was struck by the thought that soon he'd be back in the building, staying in his office overnight. It was a nice office, of course. Luxury accommodations by almost any standards. But what made her sad about it was the fact that he was staying at the office because he wasn't going to be in Chicago long.

He was leaving. Again.

As soon as Evan's car's taillights were out of sight, Meredith put hers in Park and put her head in her hands. This was so much harder than she'd thought it would be. Her nerves were not as strong as they usually were.

Neither was her willpower, come to think of it.

What a fool she was to keep having these romantic leanings toward Evan Hanson. For heaven's sake, he'd left her, abandoned her. Made promises he'd clearly had no intention of keeping, and when faced with the challenge of standing up and being a man against his father, or running away, he'd chosen to run.

Okay, that was then and this was now. The fact remained that Evan had always been a wild kid. It was as if he was incapable of following the rules. She'd seen it in school, then she'd seen it again when he ran away from his promise of commitment.

Guys like that didn't change. People like that didn't change, she amended.

And if being with Evan now was going to create this rush of longing in her, then she was just going to have to avoid him. As hard as that might be.

She drove home in silence, not daring to turn on the radio for fear of hearing some old love song that would make her feel even more melancholy. What was wrong with her? Why was she suddenly feeling so hung up on Evan Hanson again?

It wasn't the Evan Hanson of the past that she was wanting, either, it was Evan today. Past Evan was the main obstacle, that was for sure. She couldn't trust the today Evan because of what he'd done before, and it didn't look as if she was ever going to get a satisfactory resolution to that.

And frankly, she felt like an idiot for even trying.

She got home and went inside, hating the emptiness of the house and the way her footsteps echoed on the hardwood floors. Once upon a time she'd crept across these floors on tiptoe in the middle of the night, trying to avoid the creakiest boards so she didn't wake her parents up.

Now she could jump and yell and sing "The

Star Spangled Banner" if she wanted to and no one would come.

It was lonely.

And it hadn't struck her that way until Evan had returned. She hated how much she loved being with him, and more than that she hated how alone she felt every time he left.

She couldn't wait until this job was over so she could move on. That he was staying temporarily in his office with the intention of leaving himself should only make her feel better.

She took out a key and went to the back room, where she'd locked her confidential work files. She found them, carried the folders into the kitchen and spread the information out on the counter.

Then she picked up the phone and dialed.

"Okay, I'm home," she said when the line was answered. "And I've got the information you need. Are you ready?"

Chapter Fourteen

Evan knew he shouldn't go back to Meredith's house.

He knew, even as he turned the car onto Lake Shore Drive and headed across town, that it was a mistake.

What they had was in the past and, considering the fact that they couldn't even talk about it at all without arguing, it was going to have to stay there.

But he was drawn to her. Not as the boy was drawn to the spunky cheerleader, but as the man was drawn to the woman. She was the realization of everything he'd ever wanted in a woman and hadn't been able to find.

The only problem was that they had a past.

And that was precisely why it was so foolish of him to be retracing his steps down that path right now, parking outside the house she'd lived in with her parents, walking up the same walk, over the same cracks that had been there for years, going to the same door that would open to reveal the girl of his dreams.

Somehow he had to convince her of that.

He wasn't quite at the door yet when he caught sight of her through the window. She was sitting on a bar stool in the kitchen, the phone to her ear, poring over what looked like maps spread out on the counter.

Evan stepped back and watched her for a moment. He remembered the way she'd pushed that chestnut-colored hair back off her face, and the way the front of her hair bent from being constantly pushed back or tucked behind her ear.

He smiled when she laughed into the phone and tossed her head back.

She was so pretty.

He didn't know how long he stood there, or what he hoped to achieve. Maybe to talk himself out of going to the front door. But the more he watched her, the closer he wanted to get to her.

She ran a pen down the paper and spoke into the phone, looking very serious. At one point she stopped, frowned and looked through another pile before triumphantly producing whatever it was she was looking for.

He'd seen her like this in the library of Showell High School and in the offices of Hanson Media Group. Meredith was a woman who took great pleasure in a job well done, whether the job was a term paper, a report or finding a telephone number someone had asked for.

He found that brand of concentration particularly endearing on her.

When she hung up the phone and started to collect her papers, he didn't even take the time to think things through. He just strode to the door and knocked.

For several moments he stood there, wondering if she'd heard and if he should still turn and leave as if he'd never been there.

He'd almost convinced himself to do just that when she opened the door.

"Evan!"

A thousand things ran through his mind. A

million explanations, a billion apologies. But it all boiled down to one salient point.

"I was a fool."

She looked puzzled. "What?"

He stepped toward her, and she opened the door and stepped back, allowing him in. "I had no idea what I was giving up when I left here."

"Evan, have you been drinking?"

He laughed. "Not a drop. In fact, I'm more sober than I've been in years."

She closed the door and stood her ground, even when he took another step toward her.

He looked down into her beautiful face and wished he could erase every stress line he or his family had put there. But then again, he liked the gentle lines on her face. He liked the new maturity there. He liked everything about the way she looked.

"I didn't know how to betray my father, and the only way I could think of to avoid betraying you was to leave. To remove myself from the equation altogether. I thought you'd be better off. And I honestly thought—" he sighed "—I thought you'd forget all about me in no time and that it wouldn't matter."

She swallowed. "I never forgot."

He shook his head. "Neither did I. And that

was the worst error in judgment I made. Because I also thought that someday *I'd* forget, too. Everything everyone says about young love—that it's fleeting, that you remember it later with a smile and a little embarrassment but no heartache, that it never lasts. All of that was untrue."

Her eyes were shining with unshed tears. "We shouldn't be talking about this."

"I know, but *not* talking about it isn't working, either."

"I know." She sniffed.

"Look, you can tell me to go to hell." He gave a dry laugh and shook his head. "I wouldn't blame you one bit for that. But I at least want you to understand that, whatever my stupid and misguided reasons for leaving, I never *ever* stopped loving you."

He heard her breath catch in her throat. "Then why did you *stay* away? Why, when you realized how you felt, didn't you come back? Or contact me somehow?"

"Because all I knew was how I felt and that I'd let you down. I couldn't imagine that you would be willing to talk to me."

She shook her head.

"And honestly, Meredith," he went on, "I

could imagine, all too easily, that you'd moved on and forgotten us."

"You didn't have much faith in me."

"No," he said firmly. "I didn't have much faith in *me*. And, hell, I didn't deserve it."

They stood looking at each other in silence for a long, shuddering moment.

"No," she said at last. "You didn't."

He accepted that.

He had to.

"You're right," he agreed. "I just wanted you to know the truth." He started to leave.

"Why?" she asked behind him.

He stopped and turned back to face her. "What?"

"*Why* did you want me to know the truth? Why now, after all this time? In fact, why now after the nonconversation we had about this earlier tonight?"

"Because even though we'd like to be mature people who don't sweat this kind of thing, it's been the elephant in the room ever since we started working together. It was starting to spill over into everything I did, everything I thought about."

"So you needed to get it off your chest," she challenged. "To relieve your conscience."

"Mer, it would take a noble explanation for

leaving to relieve my conscience," he said earnestly. "That's not gonna happen. The reason I wanted to tell you this is because you deserved to know it because it's the truth. I love you, Meredith. I always have. And, God help me, I guess I always will." He gave a small smile. "That's the last I'll say about it, though, don't worry. Good night, Meredith."

He turned to leave and had taken two steps toward the door when she said, "Evan, wait. Don't go."

She should have let him go, but she couldn't.

She ran to him, and it all happened as if in slow motion. He turned to her, she threw herself into his arms, and they kissed. Long and deeply, and expressing all of the unanswered passion they had felt for all this time but had been unable to share.

Wordlessly she took his hand and led him up the stairs to her bedroom. He didn't ask questions. He didn't need to.

They stopped in the doorway of her bedroom and kissed again.

"Not the same room you used to have," Evan murmured.

"That would be just too weird, wouldn't it?" She smiled at him, and they kissed again.

He moved his hands up her back in tantalizing slow motion, moving his fingertips across her back so lightly she arched against him when it tickled. When she did, he unhooked her bra with one quick flick of his fingers.

She remembered that move.

The fabric fell loose and he pressed his palms against her back, drawing her closer to him still. She went willingly, eagerly. If she could have, she would have gone right into his soul.

They kissed for long minutes, maybe ten or fifteen of them, unhurried but both certain where this was going.

Just as Meredith began to feel as if her core was melting into a puddle at her feet, he whispered, "Let's move to the bed."

She didn't argue.

They crossed the room and fell to the bed together, resuming their kiss and increasing the urgency. Evan yanked at Meredith's shirt and it flew open, the buttons popping off and clattering to the floor like pennies. She didn't care. The sooner he touched her, the *more* he touched her, the better.

His hand skidded across her rib cage to her breast, his touch hot against her skin. He moved his hand to her nipple, playing her like an instrument, until her breath came in short, shallow bursts, her heart pounding urgently, begging for satisfaction.

She cupped her hands to his face and kissed him deeply, then moved her hands down the length of his chest and the flat of his stomach, until she got to the buckle of his jeans.

She hadn't forgotten her own moves, either, and she dipped her hand inside his pants, and snapped them open as Evan groaned against her mouth.

"If you're going to stop this, you'd better do it, like, five minutes ago," he said against her mouth.

"I'm not sure…." She smiled and kissed him again, enjoying the game.

Apparently, he was, too. He slid his hand inside her pants and cupped her, dipping one finger into her womanhood for just a moment. "No?"

She gasped. "I guess we could keep going." She moved her own hand to hold him. She was awed by the power of his desire and it made her crazy with her own, but she tried to sound controlled. "Unless you want to stop…?"

"You play dirty."

"You don't seem to mind." She moved her hand, looking into his eyes. "Do you?"

Evan finally lost the control he'd been holding on to. He rolled her over onto her back and slid her pants down, his breath traveling hotly across her thighs as he did so. She reminded herself that this was Evan, that this was the love of her life, and finally—*finally*—she was going to feel him within her again.

She'd waited a long time for this, even while she'd told herself she didn't want it.

All of her thoughts disappeared when Evan took her to new heights of pleasure.

"You're amazing," she breathed.

"You ain't seen nothin' yet," he said, with a pirate's smile.

He moved over her, and she couldn't wait any longer. She pushed his jeans down over his slender hips with her feet and pulled him on top of her. She wanted him.

She *needed* him.

She ran her hands across his tightly muscled backside, then around to the front, where she found him more than ready for her.

Their tongues moved against each other, echoing the drumbeat that was pounding within them. They were like a well-oiled machine whose sole purpose was to join their bodies and move them toward ecstasy.

She started to move, and he stopped her. "Wait," he said. "Let me. Relax."

So she did. She lay back against the cool, soft sheets and let herself sink into the magic that was making love with Evan.

His hand moved across her stomach and her muscles tightened in anticipation. He took his sweet time to move his hand lower, and lower, grazing her pelvis and slowing tantalizingly before finally cupping over the part of her that wanted him so desperately.

He paused for only a second, looking into her eyes, a moment that said more than words could, before slipping his fingers in and plunging her depths.

Meredith's hands clutched at the sheets beneath her as Evan brought her to heights she'd never even imagined before. She closed her eyes and let it happen, feeling waves of warm and cold wash over her while she writhed under his careful ministrations. She could barely breathe. Every time she reached the brink, he backed off, until finally he allowed her release.

With perfect timing, Evan lowered his weight onto her, and she finally felt the satisfaction of being completely one with him.

She'd dreamed of this moment.

Breathlessly she opened her mouth, deepening their kisses. The sensation was exquisite: the weight of Evan on her, the feel of him inside her, the touch of his hands on her hair as he looked down into her eyes.

Everything felt right.

They both moaned in pleasure as her body accepted his again and again, and they moved together, slowly at first and then faster, until she heard him hold his breath for a moment, then give one final thrust as she felt herself float into ecstasy once again.

Chapter Fifteen

Evan just lay there, watching her sleep.

He had waited a long time for this. Now that he and Meredith had finally made love again, it was clear to him that all the other women he'd met along the way had paled in comparison to Meredith.

He didn't know how long he watched her—it may have been an hour or more—but finally he decided to take a break and get a drink of water. It had been a long, exhausting night and he was thirsty.

He crept down the stairs and went into the

kitchen. Everything was still in the same place. Glasses in the cabinet to the right of the stove, cold water in a pitcher in the fridge. He poured a glass, drank it fast, then poured another one and sat down at the counter to drink it.

That was when his own name caught his eye.

The papers Meredith had been looking at earlier were still on the counter. He hadn't meant to pry—if he hadn't seen the words "Evan Hanson—wild card" from the corner of his eye, he might not have noticed them at all. Despite the fact that they had Hanson Media Group and the names of many of his family members and co-workers scrawled all over them.

> *Jack Hanson*—definite keep. Major asset, works well with Samantha.
>
> *Parker Lemming*—fishy accounting; look closer. Not sure if incompetent or dishonest.
>
> *Lily Harper*—keep for merger, very good worker, being headhunted by competition.
>
> *David Hanson*—good worker, trustworthy. Invested in own family but not to the detriment of HMG.

Marla Cooper—very promising, on the
   fast track to success. Keep her!
Andrew Hanson—on the right track, keep
   an eye on him. Looks like he'll be okay.
Stephen ?? in mail room—real possibilities. Keep and promote.
Evan Hanson—wild card.

Stephen in the mail room hadn't even needed
a last name, and she thought he had "real possibilities," but she had gone on to list pros and
cons about Evan.

Pros:
• Has Hanson name to protect.
• Capable when he puts his mind to it.
• Determined to succeed if only to prove
   everyone wrong about him.
• Is respected around the office and in the
   business, despite glaring inexperience.

Cons:
• Doesn't always seem to care if his
   father's company goes down in flames.
• Could possibly be sabotaging efforts as
   "revenge."
• No experience to see things through;

       might do some good things in starting
       up the broadcast enterprises but might
       not have the gumption to finish.
- A little immature, impulsive. Maybe not
  capable of being a professional?
- Tends to run away when the going gets
  tough.

He read the lists a couple of times, shaking
his head in disbelief. If this was what she
thought of him, why on earth had she just slept
with him?

More to the point, why was she documenting
everyone's performance at Hanson Media
Group? Why would she even care? She was a
new hire, working in the PR department, for
Pete's sake. What that had to do with Jack or
David or Samantha or Richard Warren or
anyone else, he couldn't imagine.

Except…he looked at more of the papers.
Numbers, flow charts, strengths, weaknesses,
Wall Street Journal references, the assets of the
competition and their interest in acquiring.

It all became very clear, very fast.

Meredith was a corporate spy.

The revelation was stunning. A spy.
Meredith, who had always prided herself on

being so honest. Meredith, who held honesty in others to be the most important quality. Meredith, who had just melted in his arms and made him feel like the luckiest man on earth.

Everything about her was a lie.

For a few minutes, Evan couldn't move. If he stood up, he wasn't sure which direction he'd take: out the door or upstairs to wake her and demand answers. He didn't want to do either one of those things without thinking it through first.

Why would she do this? The first reason that came to mind was revenge. She couldn't have planned on Evan coming back to work here, so her initial motivation might have been to get back at the company that had ruined her father's.

In truth, Evan could sort of understand that. He didn't particularly *admire* it, but he understood why she might have felt that way.

What he didn't understand was how she could make love to him, all the while knowing she was assisting *someone's* efforts to steal his family's company. Hell, she was even listing his own bad qualities—or what she perceived to be his bad qualities—for the same purpose.

The Meredith he knew would never have been able to have sex with someone as a way of using them to her own advantage. Or, worse, to the advantage of her employer, whoever that was.

Yet that was exactly what the woman upstairs had done.

And he wanted no part of it.

He stood up and took his glass to the sink, opening the dishwasher in what felt like slow motion. The small gesture felt ironic when balanced against the enormous amount of feeling he was battling with. He'd risked his own heart—love was always a risk—he'd take his lumps for that. Maybe he even deserved it, after what he'd done to Meredith all those years ago.

He'd think about that later.

The immediate dilemma was what to do about the deception. He'd faced this same issue once before, when his father had sabotaged her father's business, and he had done the wrong thing. A weak warning to Meredith and a mad dash out of town hadn't amounted to anything good.

This time he'd have to take definitive action. He could tell Meredith he knew what she was up to and demand answers, but she might not give them to him. And, once she was caught, someone else might be sent in her stead, and he wouldn't be so lucky as to catch the next person.

So maybe he should talk to Helen instead.

That was probably the answer. It was probably the mature and responsible thing to do. Of course, it went against everything inside him to do that, but Evan Hanson had to learn to be *mature,* as Meredith herself had noted.

He had to be *professional.*

And more than anything, at the moment he had to get out of this house.

Meredith woke as the dawn sliced through her window, feeling uncharacteristically happy. It took her a full minute or two of thinking through her groggy state to remember why.

When she did, she smiled.

"Evan?"

She wished he was in bed next to her, but he must have gotten up first. Maybe he was in the shower or downstairs making bad coffee like he used to.

She got out of bed and walked toward the bathroom. "Evan?" she called again.

The silence that answered was noticeable.

No one was here.

But that was impossible. Evan wouldn't just cut out on her after something like last night. She walked around the house looking for him, and calling his name every once in a while, finally arriving in the kitchen. Maybe he'd gone to pick up some breakfast and had left her a note.

But there was no note.

Meredith paused in the middle of the kitchen, wondering for a moment if she'd imagined the whole night. If she had, she'd done so in great and frightening detail.

But she hadn't; she knew she hadn't.

She sat down at the counter, miffed, trying to figure out where he would have gone and why he wouldn't have left a note or something.

The realization came all too quickly:

"Hanson. Hanson. Hanson Media Group. Evan Hanson. Pros. Cons."

The writing was on the wall, or at least all over the counter. All of her notes, all of her reports, all of her unflattering doodles about Evan himself, all lying right there on the counter for him to see when he got up.

Oh, God.

He'd seen it all. She didn't even have to think about it or speculate about other possible explanations for his absence. He'd seen her life laid out on the counter, figured out what she was up to, and he'd left.

What was she going to do now?

Meredith had never been good at wringing her hands and clutching her pearls in an emergency—and this was definitely an emergency—so what she decided to do was take the bull by the horns and let her employer know exactly what had happened.

There was no point in sitting around the house, hoping Evan had somehow missed the glaring evidence before him and had gone out for doughnuts.

Meredith took the quickest shower of her life, dried her hair in no time flat, skipped the make-up and got dressed for work. During that time, Evan did *not* show up again with a bag of bagels and a goofy grin, so it was pretty obvious that he was gone and not coming back.

Within forty-five minutes of realizing that Evan was gone, Meredith was in her car on the way to admit her carelessness and risk the wrath of her employer.

Evan was still struggling with the question of what to do about Meredith's spying when he got back to work.

It wasn't so easy to simply go to Helen's office and let her know. If he'd had the power to fire Meredith, he might have done so, just to spare himself and her the agony of retribution from Hanson Media Group and Helen.

He could have kicked himself for being suckered in by Meredith. Why had he believed that she felt the same way he did after all these years? After all, it was always easier for the one who stays in place—she was able to work through the grief and the loneliness. She'd moved on with her life, formed other relationships, developed her career.

Evan, on the other hand, had taken an extended vacation, working odd jobs in various places far away, and he'd never quite gotten to the point where he was able to forget her.

Certainly when he got back to Chicago, Meredith was primary in his mind. And if being back and thinking about her wasn't enough, Helen had to go and *hire* her, for Pete's sake, and have her work closely with Evan.

It was the worst kind of bad luck.

And the best kind of good luck.

It was every conflicted feeling, good and bad, rolled up into one.

The morning passed at the slowest pace of any day Evan could remember. Every time he decided it was best to let Helen know what was going on, he'd get no further than one step from his desk before he changed his mind and sat down again to reconsider the problem.

Yet when he resolved to tell Meredith what he knew, he hesitated there, too, and for much more complicated reasons: one, he didn't want another corporate spy—potentially someone he wouldn't have the luck to spot—come in her place; and two, he didn't want her to leave.

It was the latter that really tortured him. What a fool he was to want to keep Meredith around, even though he knew she was betraying both him and his family in the biggest possible way. And yet, he could almost understand why. She had a legitimate gripe against George Hanson.

And, arguably, against Evan himself.

But in mulling the situation over, again and again, he finally decided that even if she believed she had sufficient motivation for getting back at the Hansons, it was primarily because of him.

And he couldn't just sit by and let future generations of Hansons—his siblings' sons and daughters—be ruined because of what boiled down to his own mistake.

Whatever Meredith was doing, it was because of him and because of the way he and his father had treated her and her father, more than a decade back.

It was time he made things right.

Unfortunately, he wasn't going to be able to make things right for Meredith if he made things right for the company.

He was just going to have to be *mature* and *professional* about this.

Contrary to Meredith's stated opinion.

But by 4:30 p.m. he still hadn't made a move toward Helen's office to reveal what he knew about Meredith. It was one thing to intend to handle it, but actually going forward and telling was a whole different thing.

He didn't want to do it.

But when Helen summoned him to her office just before five o'clock, he realized he couldn't put it off anymore.

He was going to have to do *something*.

Chapter Sixteen

Approaching Helen's office, Evan decided that he would talk to Meredith about this privately.

Yes, his loyalty should have been with the company—especially under the circumstances—but he just couldn't turn Meredith over to the wolves like that, no matter what she'd done. It could ruin her professionally, and he just didn't want to do that.

His decision was solidified when he ran into her outside Helen's office.

"Evan," she said, startled when she looked up and saw him.

She looked as if she was leaving Helen's office. And she looked upset.

"You left so early," she went on.

Had that only been this morning? He'd spent so much time waffling back and forth on what to do about Meredith that it seemed as though it had been days instead of hours. "I had to get to work," he said.

She raised an eyebrow. "Is that all it was?"

"What else *would* it be?" he asked pointedly.

She swallowed but held his gaze without flinching. "I thought perhaps you had changed your mind about me for some reason."

"I'm not the one who's changed, Meredith."

She took a short breath, looked as if she was going to say something, then stopped.

Standing there before him, she almost looked vulnerable. And she definitely looked alluring, with her rich, shining hair hanging loose, framing her still-youthful face. Was it his imagination or did her cheeks still have some of the glow he'd seen in them after they'd made love last night?

It didn't matter. That was a mistake. One he wasn't likely to make again.

"So you're here to see Helen?" Meredith asked awkwardly.

"Yes." He nodded. "Where are you going?"

Home? Had Helen already figured her out and fired her?

"Just back to my office. David's got a lot of work piled up for me, and of course you and I have to finish the new promotional campaign."

It was crazy, but some part of him was glad to hear that she'd still be in the office. She would probably quit once he'd talked to her, but in the meantime she'd still be here.

"I'll call you when my meeting with Helen is finished," he said. "Are you still going to be around for a while?"

"I'll wait as long as I need to. I can work all night, if necessary." Her cheeks went pink and she looked down.

It was on the tip of his tongue to make a flip joke about working all night with her, and he had to remind himself that things had changed. Despite last night, he and Meredith couldn't have an easy rapport.

Tension stretched between them.

"I'd better get in there," Evan said at last, gesturing vaguely in the direction of Helen's office.

Meredith nodded and stepped back, allowing him room to pass. "I'll see you afterward," she said. Then he could have sworn she added quietly, "I hope."

He went into Helen's quiet office and closed the door behind him, settling uneasily into the seat before her.

"I'll get right to the point," Helen said to him from across her desk. "Not everything here at Hanson Media Group is what it seems."

That was for sure. But he sat back and said nothing, waiting for Helen to continue, which she did.

"Not every*one* here is as they seem."

He nodded noncommittally. "People seldom are."

"I think you know what I'm talking about, Evan."

He met her eyes. "Why don't you tell me?"

"I'm talking about Meredith Waters. She's been doing some corporate work for another company. Digging up information on Hanson Media Group to determine its viability for a merger."

"What company?"

"TAKA Corporation."

"The Japanese conglomerate?" He'd done some homework on his industry. Enough to know that TAKA was enormous.

Helen nodded. "That's right."

"And you're not upset about this?"

She folded her hands on the desk in front of

her and looked her stepson straight in the eye. "No, Evan. I sought TAKA out and proposed a merger to them."

It took a long moment of silence for that to sink in, and even then he couldn't quite believe he'd heard her correctly.

"I'm sorry," he said. "I don't think I understand."

She took a short breath and hesitated a moment before explaining. "I don't like the idea of sharing Hanson's power with anyone. I don't want to change the structure this company has had for so many years. Your father worked hard to build this empire, and I wish it could just go on without him, exactly as he'd envisioned."

Evan was surprised by her vehemence and her support for George. "You really loved him, didn't you?"

"Yes. And I respect what he built. But times have changed since Hanson first gained power. There are too many media outlets today, it's hard to monopolize, and if a company can't monopolize, it runs the risk of going under completely."

"Which is what you were afraid of when we first talked about me staying on and trying to help you keep in business."

"Exactly." She nodded. "And it's what I'm still afraid of. If Hanson doesn't get a boost of some sort, it's *going* to fold. And TAKA's interest might be just the boost we need." She leaned back in her chair and sighed. "The truth is, no other company has expressed even the slightest interest in a merger."

"So TAKA is our only hope."

She nodded again. "It looks like it."

"They're getting pretty specific information, from what I could tell. Lots of financial-risk stuff. What if they want a takeover instead of a merger? Then Hanson is lost just as much as if it had gone bankrupt. Maybe even more."

"I won't allow a takeover of this company," Helen said firmly. "I assure you of that. In fact, you can see for yourself. I would like you to go to Japan with me right away for a meeting with Ichiro Kobayashi. He needs reassurance on your latest hire, Lenny Doss, and I'd feel better if you gave it to him in person. Now that everything's out in the open."

Now he was going to Japan? What the heck—it wasn't much weirder than anything else that had happened lately. "Fine."

"I'm leaving tomorrow. Can I have Sonia make a reservation for you to join me?"

He nodded and spread his arms. "I'm at your disposal."

She buzzed Sonia and asked her to make plane and hotel reservations for Evan. He waited, trying to process all this new information.

When she hung up the phone, she smiled at him. "Thank you, Evan. I know this is all sudden and surprising, but I think it's for the best. Perhaps after you've met with TAKA yourself, you'll be able to help me persuade everyone else that this is the right move."

"We'll see." He considered his next question before asking it. "So TAKA comes along and expresses an interest in merging with Hanson. You decide you're not completely averse to the idea. What I want to know is, where does Meredith fit in? Did you uncover her double dealings and get the truth out of her?"

"No." Helen gave a small chuckle and shook her head. "No, it was nothing like that. Meredith is here digging up all the relevant information for TAKA because I hired her."

Evan went back to his office more confused than he'd been when he left it. Two months ago he'd been as far away from this company and this lifestyle as he could get, and now suddenly he was right smack in the middle of it all: black ink, red ink, mergers, takeovers and corporate espionage.

He could really use a shot of tequila right about now.

Instead it was just more of the same. He got to the office he was beginning to resent, sat down at the desk he was beginning to hate and called the woman he was beginning to love.

Meredith appeared within five minutes, looking pale and drawn. "Did Helen tell you... what's going on?"

"That you're a spy for TAKA?" Evan asked casually. "Yes, she mentioned that."

"But you knew that."

He gave a concessionary shrug. "I knew you were spying for someone."

Her eyes grew bright. "Evan, I'm really sorry I couldn't tell you. But it's my job to be discreet. If I'd let on what I was doing, it could have compromised all of Helen's plans."

"Assuming I couldn't be trusted."

She winced. "I didn't know. I still don't know. I understand that you're mad that I lied to you, and I don't blame you for that, but I don't know where you stand on the truth."

He gave a half shrug. "Well, that makes two of us."

"You see, don't you?" She moved toward him and leaned on the desk, next to where he sat. "You see why I couldn't let on."

"In theory, I suppose. But in practice…I'm not so sure. Was last night part of your work or was it extracurricular?"

It took her a moment to realize what he was asking, and he could see when it registered. Her eyes grew wide and flashing mad. "Are you asking me if I *slept* with you to get information about the company?"

Man, it sounded harsh when put that way. "I'm wondering what last night was for you, Meredith, and how it fit into your plans to assist in a takeover of my family's company."

Her eyes burned with anger. "If Helen told you what was going on, then she told you that this merger is the only way to save the company. If anything, my efforts will *help* your family, not hurt it."

"So this was altruistic of you."

"No, this was a job for me." She raised her chin defiantly. "It didn't matter to me what Helen wanted the information for. She asked me to get it and I did."

"So—"

"But," she interrupted, "as soon as I did, she made me aware of her intentions and the fact that she was doing this for the good of your company and your family. So by the time last night came along, I was well aware that I was not hurting you or your father's company, though he may have richly deserved it once."

She was right. He knew she was right. Her rationale was completely legitimate. How could he argue with it?

He stood up, standing over her, but she didn't move, didn't flinch. "Did last night have anything to do with your work on this potential merger?"

"No," she answered evenly. "Did we even *talk* about business last night? As a matter of fact, did I ask you to come over last night or did you just show up on your own?"

Good point. "Maybe you planned it."

"Not unless I'm psychic."

"Maybe you took a chance on getting it right."

"Then I wouldn't have been stupid enough to leave the evidence out for you to find, would I? Or I wouldn't have been stupid enough to fall asleep and let you wander the house and find my supposedly secret evidence."

Hard to argue with that one. "Then why did you do it, knowing that you were plotting against the company?"

She looked exasperated. "Number one, I wasn't plotting *against* anyone, and number two, it had nothing to do with work. At least for me it didn't." She shifted her weight, changing to a more combative posture. "What about you? What was *your* motivation, Evan?"

"Mine… My motivation was—" He pulled her closer and lowered his lips onto hers. The heat of the desire that washed over him was a surprise, even though he'd been feeling it in every inter-action with her since she'd joined the company.

This was bad.

"It doesn't matter," he finished lamely. "Look, I've got to go. I'm flying to Japan to-morrow with Helen to meet with your bosses. I need to get some rest."

"They're not my bosses," Meredith objected. "Helen is. Same as you."

His head was spinning. The only thing he knew for sure was that he couldn't continue this conversation right now.

"They might be all of our bosses pretty soon," Evan said. "Now I have to go and make sure that's in the best interest of the family."

"And the company."

"The company *is* the family," he said, feeling it for the first time in his life. "Now, is there anything you can tell me that would help me in my conversations with TAKA?"

She nodded. "That the broadcasting division is already up, thanks to the announcements of Lenny Doss's addition. You made a good decision there. That will snag a good portion of the eighteen to thirty-four demographic. Dr. Ebony Lyle, airing in the afternoons, will pick up women in the same age group. And the Sports Addicts have a primarily male audience from eighteen to sixty-three. You've done really well," she concluded.

So had she. He hated to admit it, but he was really impressed with the facts she had at the ready.

In fact, he was impressed with just about everything Meredith did. But that wasn't a surprise to him. She'd always been capable and smart and creative.

The thing she hadn't always been was part of his daily life. For twelve years, though he remembered her frequently, he'd managed to live without her from day to day.

Now he wasn't so sure he could do that. He

found he wanted her around more and more, that he'd look for her even when he knew she wasn't there, and he'd listen for her voice on the wind.

He needed her around him.

He was a better man with her around.

Worse, he felt incomplete without her. And that scared him to death.

Chapter Seventeen

There was a silence in the TAKA offices that was unlike anything Evan had ever experienced. It gave him the creeps. Back home the Hanson offices were bustling, even though there were empty offices these days. But TAKA ran like a smooth engine, no bangs or dings, just a quiet hum.

Evan and Helen sat in the executive office with Richard Warren, Helen's attorney, discussing details of the merger.

When Evan was called upon to address the issues surrounding the broadcasting division, he answered all of the questions easily. Evan wouldn't have imagined he'd be so comfortable with corporate parlance but he was.

After the meeting was over, Richard and Evan stood in the hallway talking.

"I'm concerned that they mentioned the word *takeover,*" Evan said. "Is that a language idiosyncrasy or are they thinking takeover instead of merger?"

Richard took a short breath. "I don't know. I'm concerned about the same thing."

That didn't make Evan feel any better. "I wonder what Helen's take on this is." He saw her from the corner of his eye. "Helen—"

The woman who stopped and looked at him wasn't Helen. She had copper-colored hair, for one thing, and was a couple of decades younger than Helen. Evan did a double take, then said, "Sorry, I thought you were someone else."

Finally Helen did appear, and when she did Evan was glad to see her. "Is TAKA looking for a takeover instead of a merger?" he asked her.

"*I'm* looking for a merger," she said firmly. "And your coming and telling them about Hanson's assets has really helped in that pursuit. Thank you."

"I hope it helped," Evan said uncertainly.

"It did." Helen was completely confident. "Believe me. Things are definitely going the way I want them to."

They got back to the office late at night. Because Evan had stopped to get something to eat on the way home, Helen had gotten back to Hanson Media Group some time before he did.

When he arrived, she seemed to be the only one in the office.

Helen stopped him on his way to his office. "You've got to talk to Meredith."

"What?"

"She's here and she's trying to resign," Helen said.

"Resign?" he repeated, numb. "Why?"

"Because she sees herself as an impediment to your comfort here. She talked about how well you're doing and how she doesn't want to get in the way of that."

"But she's got so much to do with how well I'm doing."

Helen nodded. "She's been an asset for sure."

Something about the way she said it gave Evan pause. "You knew, didn't you?"

She assumed a blank expression. Too blank. "Knew what?"

"About Meredith and me. You knew about our past. That's why you threw us together."

"Meredith and you are both good workers, and you worked well together," she said, but her momentary glance at the floor told him everything he needed to know.

"You can't make up for everything my father did to all of us," Evan said quietly.

She gave a shrug and a small smile. "But I can help make up for some of it."

He shook his head and gave her a hug. "You're too much. I wish I'd met you years ago."

She looked pleased. "I do, too. Now get back into Meredith's office and stop her from leaving. I've got to go now, and the cleaning crew has already been here, so that will leave you two alone." She said it pointedly. "So remember to lock up when and if you leave." She didn't wait for an answer, just gave him a coy smile and a wink before leaving.

He hurried to Meredith's office. He stopped at the door and watched her putting things from her desk into a box in sad, slow motion.

"What do you think you're doing?" he asked her.

"I've got a new job."

"No, you don't. You just want to get away from this one."

"That's not true."

"Helen told me." He walked toward her. "She told me a lot, in fact. Did you know she knew about us before hiring either one of us?"

Meredith's face registered such genuine surprise that he knew immediately that she'd had no idea. "She set us up?"

He took her hands in his. "I'm afraid so. What's worse, she predicted what would happen exactly."

"What happened?" she asked, looking into his eyes.

"We fell in love again."

"You...? Are you saying you *love* me?"

"Baby, I've *always* loved you. I'm saying I've finally realized it."

Meredith's breath caught in her throat. "So you really don't want me to leave?"

"If you do, I'm leaving, too." He smiled. "And you know how hard it is to pull me out of corporate America."

She gave a laugh. "So what do we do?"

"Glad you asked," he said, and lowered his mouth to hers.

The moment their lips touched he felt as if an

electric shock jolted through him from her. He tightened his fingers on her shoulders and pulled her closer, willing her to stay with him, in this moment, and not to pull back and call it a mistake.

Evan hovered, just for a moment, with his lips almost touching hers. Their breath mingled and Meredith found herself trembling. He asked, "How do you like my plan so far?"

"So far it works for me."

Never in his life had Evan felt such a tsunami of desire. The kiss went from hungry to gentle, then back to hungry again. For long moments they backed off, lips barely touching, teasing, inviting more.

Her scent was heady up close—sweet and floral with just a hint of the familiar.

Meredith lifted a hand to his five-o'clock-shadow-roughened cheek and ran her fingertips across the contours of his face, her small hand soft against him.

Neither of them could find the words: all they had was the motion.

Evan ran his hands down her back, and she arched toward him, her pelvis pressed against his increasing arousal.

He wanted her.

In one fast motion, he pushed everything off her desk, the hell with the mess. Then he slowly lowered her to the desktop and positioned himself over her.

She let herself mold beneath him, allowing his body to dictate the direction they'd take. She countered his every movement with a complementary movement of her own.

Evan's arms tightened around her waist, and he kissed her more, trailing kisses along her jaw and down to her shoulder.

"So does this mean you forgive me for lying?" she asked, breathless against his neck.

"Only if you forgive me for every stupid thing I ever did."

"That could take a while," she responded with a giggle. "I hope you've got time."

"All the time in the world." He pulled closer.

She lifted her arms to rest on his shoulders, and tangled her fingers in his hair. "Promise me we'll never part again."

"I promise." He moved his hands across her body and kissed her sweetly. Her lips opened under his and he deepened the kiss, aroused by the semifamiliar taste of her. It had been a long time and she'd certainly gained experience since he'd last been with her, yet there was something about her that felt not only familiar but also right.

He ran his hands slowly down her sides, then drew them around her waist, pulling her closer still, pressing her against his own desire for her.

Meredith slid her hands down his shoulders and sides, slowly, as if she knew that every small fraction of an inch raised his desire. Indeed, he felt as if he came alive under her touch. These were feelings she hadn't enjoyed in years.

She wasn't even sure she'd *ever* felt them before.

All she knew was that the moment she'd first laid eyes on Evan again, despite the fact that twelve bitter years had passed, she'd felt something drawing her to him.

Now she suspected he felt the same.

Meredith trailed her hands across his stomach then flattened her palms against his chest, his skin warm against hers, making what almost felt like fire.

Evan eased his hands down to the small of her back. She felt beautiful. Her body molded softly against his and he felt warm, despite the fact that the office air-conditioning was on full blast.

When he finally eased himself into her and

satiated her longing, she felt as if she'd been given water after four days of dying from thirst. This was no longer about the personal pleasure—it was about survival. And, with Evan—at least for the moment—she had found a way to survive this crazy life she was living.

With Evan she knew she could survive anything.

* * * * *

Look for the next installment of the new
Special Edition continuity,
THE FAMILY BUSINESS
HER BEST-KEPT SECRET
by Brenda Harlen

Attorney Richard Warren never expected to
meet the love of his life on a business trip.
Then reporter Jenny Anderson captured his
heart the day they met. But a secret in Jenny's
past threatens to tear them apart....
On sale May 2006, wherever
Silhouette Books are sold.

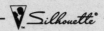

SPECIAL EDITION™

Bound by fate, a shattered family renews
their ties—and finds a legacy of love.

Family
BUSINESS

HER BEST-KEPT SECRET

by Brenda Harlen

Jenny Anderson had always known
she was adopted. But a fling-turned-serious
with Hanson Media Group attorney
Richard Warren brought her closer than ever
to the truth about her past. In his arms,
would she finally find the love she's
always dreamed of?

Available in May 2006
wherever Silhouette books are sold.

SPECIAL EDITION™

BABY BONDS

A new miniseries by
Karen Rose Smith coming this May

THE SERIES BEGINS WITH
CUSTODY FOR TWO

Shaye Bartholomew had always wanted a child,
and now she was guardian for her friend's
newborn. Then the infant's uncle showed up,
declaring Timmy belonged with him.

Could one adorable baby forge a
family bond between them?

*And don't miss
THE BABY TRAIL,
available in July.*

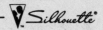

SPECIAL EDITION™

WHAT SHOULD HAVE BEEN

by *Helen R. Myers*

May 2006

A grave injury had erased Delta Force soldier Mead Regan's memory—until a chance encounter with first love Devan Anderson, now widowed and raising a daughter, brought everything back. Could they stake a new claim on life together, or would Mead's meddling mother make this a short-lived reunion?

Look for WHAT SHOULD HAVE BEEN wherever Silhouette Books are sold.

If you enjoyed what you just read,
then we've got an offer you can't resist!

Take 2 bestselling
love stories FREE!
Plus get a FREE surprise gift!

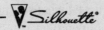

SPECIAL EDITION™

THE COWBOYS OF
COLD CREEK

Love on the ranch!

NEW FROM

RaeAnne Thayne

DANCING IN THE MOONLIGHT

May 2006

U.S. Army Reserves nurse Magdalena Cruz returned to her family's Cold Creek ranch from Afghanistan, broken in body and spirit. Now it was up to physician Jake Dalton to work his healing magic on her heart....

Read more about the dashing Dalton men:
Light the Stars, April 2006
Dalton's Undoing, June 2006

You're never too old to sneak out at night

BJ thinks her younger sister, Iris, needs a love interest. So she does what any mature woman would do and organizes an Over-Fifty Singles Night. When her matchmaking backfires it turns out to be the best thing either of them could have hoped for.

Over 50's Singles Night

by Ellyn Bache

COMING NEXT MONTH